MW01659659

# VISUAL EYES ©

An intimate Portrait.

Written By:

Marsha Reid

Copyright © 2002
Marsha Reid

All rights reserved. No part of this book may be reproduced in any form, except for the inclusion of brief quotations in a review, without permission in writing from the author or publisher.

ISBN: 0-9721415-0-2

Printed in the United States by Morris Publishing
3212 East Highway 30
Kearney, NE 68847
1-800-650-7888

Acknowledgments:

Thanks to my children, who gave me the strength to follow my heart and dreams, through the spark of unconditional love in their eyes.

Thanks to my best friend, Deatra Taylor, who's personality shines like a shooting star, for opening her heart and home to me.

Thanks to Cortina Owens for her friendship, for giving me the encouragement to mark this piece with my own unique voice, and for opening her ears to my thoughts.

Thanks to Joselyn Turner, one of my revealed allies, for your thoughts and ideas, and for the energy that caused the calculator on your desk to move on its own when we talked about my dreams.

To Kim Crain for reminding me that this feat was possible. Every time I thought about giving it up, I thought about the day you said that to me with great sincerity.

To Jason, my mysterious friend whose eye over my shoulder from time to time, helped me to accept that I will encounter an overwhelming response of disbelief.

# Preface

## In Loving Memory

My Mother, an Avid Poker Player

&

My Father, the Greatest Philosopher of My Time

"Mama, your game was always dealer's choice. When it was time for you to deal, I'd hear you say Jacks are better. So why do trips get the win? I know a king and queen don't count as a pair. Even if the joker is wild, it's not a good pair. I'll hold on to this ace of a heart you gave me, because even with a wild joker, I can make my pair. Call my hand if you will, I call it right and definitely real."

At a young age my father offered me a lesson about telling the difference between a genuine friend and an imitation. He said, "Your mind and soul are both part of your world. If you have the slightest doubt about trusting another person, the answer will always, without fail be no, and don't. Always surround yourself with people you can trust and be yourself around."

I leashed on to his advice which took the super glue effect on my mind. His concept has been a mine of gold for me. The choices of friends I made given that advice, has left me without a regretted selection. Every time I contemplate those few words when a person crosses my path, and a yes is earned, a very true friendship is gained.

I also use this same philosophy in my relationships with men. Forgive me for thinking in realistic terms, but relationships are serious to me. Although I have gained through the learning process, and find myself more cautious and aware, I make every attempt to exempt myself from the rule that makes a person judge new people, based on old experiences.

When rationalizing with myself about the day I do dive into a long term romance, it might sound silly, but I want it to be like Cinderella. I know there is no perfect person, but I know my taste, what best fits me, and above all what is comfortable to me. Like a hand in glove, the mate to the soul is where the comfort lies. If something doesn't fit, I'm not about to force it.

If I find myself feeling that right vibe, and can't see the relationship going from idle, forward, I'm not too proud to bow out. I have a limit, and the ticket I give for that violation is a suggestion that we both walk. There is no need to force a drive. Time is too precious to waste.

I will not wake up to a substitute every day, knowing the doubt will never go away. No one can convince me that it is right to state claim of a person you doubt. I am very mental and want a spiritual connection. If I go mental and let my spirit do the walking, I know the ultimate zone of comfort will be reached. This most logical life search sees no road block and knows no doors, everything is always open.

Don't get the wrong idea and don't forget to study. I give no passing scores to a man who doesn't practice selection and discretion when giving other opportunity a place on their welcome mat. Other women who are interested in the same man as I, strikes off a sense of competition, not jealousy. I as a woman, love who I am. I am not intimidated by the qualities another woman possesses. No two women are alike, and I know that I too, have plenty of good qualities.

So why do the kings and queens of the world get angry with their perspective mate because they find they have more in common with another? I don't want to be chosen by a man for keeps sake unless I am the prize they choose and I am ready to accept the crown. Why feel like you can not or should not pursue a connection because you are casually spoken for? You might be turning down a match made in heaven.

When I look around I see many relationships failing. I witness misery living in so many hearts. So many people are denied happiness because they give too much all too suddenly. They find themselves imprisoned in a relationship based on all the wrong reasons. The superficial belief that things will get to the point of greater satisfaction later, is a fairy tale. I refuse to take that kind of trip. I will not be held hostage. I will not feel obligated, nor do I want my perspective mate to.

In realistic terms I know me, I am a writer, a space person. I must have my own time. That doesn't mean that I don't care or that I don't feel the vibe, it just happens to be part of who I am. The time I spend away from a relationship is productive and essential for my mind. I hope to always have these hands to express my talent through this art. I am a soul searcher, a sole searcher.

By preference I have never tied the knot. I will not have a man sleeping here today, until I know my search will end tomorrow. Maybe this sacrifice is extreme, but constant emotional and physical comfort is not necessary for me. I might desire the fairy tale, but I refuse to live in a world of make believe. I am not living for pretend, so I do not love for pretend.

Most men find me intimidating, too independent and too good to be true. I have a wacky sense of humor, and sarcastic, but undoubtedly true advice. To make it simple, I am a most self assured extrovert. I know that there are few people who can see my innocence. I am convinced this disillusion is because my character traits are so visible. The truth is when it comes to the personal side of me, I am totally shy.

My ways may have cost me several relationships. Last summer I wanted to take a chance with an old friend who lived hundreds of miles away. How perfect was that? I couldn't ask for more space. I wanted to ante up with this brother. His hand, I found inviting and I know he holds a nice heart. I was disappointed when the hand folded. I hungered for the challenge of a perceived dog, because this kitty may've held his jackpot.

I expect my knight to have slightly rusted armor. I have rust remover ready for the right time. I can also accept stains that won't go away. If the time never comes for me to try new prospects on for size, and if my rare style is never found, I will continue to rest in my own self peace, at every midnight stroke.

If my philosophy of giving a man all the space he desires, ownership of his decisions, and control to the key to his heart is wrong, I don't want to be right. The day a key is handed off should be in the form of a proposal, a question asked and an acceptance made, making the beginning new for the process of sharing life.

My ways may require some sacrifice, but nevertheless, I still need what's missing to make my pair, the mate to the soul, in order to walk comfortably in that zone of eternal love I know is real. Happiness is something we all should feel. Call it what you will, I call it right and definitely real.

# Chapter 1

*I am walking down a long corridor with my arm around a tall man. When I turn to see who he is, I am refrained by a force pushing my head away so that I cannot see his face. My sister-in-law is standing at the end of the hallway. I ask her who he is. She says she cannot tell me. I walk with the mystery man into an arena type atmosphere and he disappears. I am looking down at the events going on below. Later, I join the mystery man in a room where we hug and kiss. I still cannot see his face.*

My eyes opened and closed again while I replayed the dream in my mind. I kicked around in the paisley print comforter wrapped around my body. The white mini blinds rustled as grueling winds stirred in the night. I reached for my dream journal on the night stand, propped myself up on my elbow and recorded the dream I titled, The Mystery Man.

The street light shined in a purple ray that reflected tiny stripes on the small bedroom. Clothes were scattered as if a thief had ransacked looking for a fortune. My luggage lined the pale green walls, framing the room with the look of a vacationer's temporary space.

Dozing in and out, constant thoughts of my move back to Illinois flooded my thoughts. Having spent the last seven weeks in Florida, the results of my efforts had proved to be nothing more than a great getaway. I rolled on my back and looked up toward the ceiling, trying to justify a move back to hell. Feeling very restless, I twirled my hair around my fingers.

It was late July when Florida weather, normally hot and heated, was dampened by a quick shower that was sure to turn the coming day into a dry, hot, roasting oven. The atmosphere for a good night's sleep was at its best, but my constant thoughts preventing me from taking advantage of the priceless event.

My step out of Illinois was driven by faith. I knew my belief system was strong, even though I never frequented church. Like my father, I have deep meditation sessions as a religious practice. Not many people can understand my philosophy on making it work without the routine of normal worship. Through meditation I gained an inner strength, and strong spiritual connection. I knew I had found my channel; my goal was to keep it locked, and to stay tuned.

Dreaming is a big part of who I am. In my adulthood I grew to know that dreaming gave me definition, especially after having dreams that could not logically be explained. I kept a journal of them, and they often held a hidden story about my life. I knew I had unlocked the magic inside that defined writing as a gifted talent, and perhaps my seed of purpose.

I am a twinless twin who always felt as if a part of me was missing, but because of it, I had a spark that ignited a centerness about me, like a knowing. Blessings in my life were countless.

The time in Florida had allowed me the opportunity to mourn the loss my parents. I had suppressed the urge to stay strong for everyone else. My dad, Bobby Cooper, passed on two years ago, and my mom Bertha, only a year ago. I had been determined my faith was strong enough to take a step out on, surely God would carry me when it became necessary. I wanted nothing more than to make God proud, after all there was no one here for me to lean on.

Before leaving Illinois, I created a play series for at-risk teenagers. I called my creation Mix-In-Motion. It is a lyrical mix, I put into motion, in the form of a situation comedy. I knew how wrapped up teens were into music, so I wanted to give them an opportunity to work while they learned about the world, using the words that intrigued them. My goal was to market my art while I worked to pay the bills.

It had seemed the resources in Florida could lay the groundwork, not to mention it is a desirable place to reside. The warm weather was a plus but the money to be made was obscure to say the least, and to make ends meet where my experience came in was virtually impossible.

Professionally I was not challenged enough. Everywhere I went, my limited educational background landed me entry level positions, but not regrettably. I learned how to master the game of life at a young age. My father was famous for planting seeds, and I paid close attention to his lessons. I knew his motivation was to make the transition to adulthood an easy one, and it worked for me. His strong words wore on my mind, and found permanent dwelling inside, giving me a sense of visualization, and determination. I was so easily able to flip the switch, that proving my self worth in record time was a simple task. I reached the potential heights almost everywhere, using my clever mind, intellectual accent, and skilled demeanor.

Mentally I felt a hunger for substantial challenges and drastic change. Physically I groomed myself fit though regular workouts. Spiritually I was still feeding and growing through constant prayer and deep meditation. My heart was in my writing, and I waited for that seed to hint an indication of what aspect in life my unique words could make a difference.

At home and in recreation I was a far different creature, one with as many flavors as Life Savers. I despised any and everything with a designer label. I was an original with a style all my own. My ranges in behavior and fashion allowed me to portray an innocent girl with a wholesome appeal, and be so bold in my attire that heads would seem to turn completely around from every angle. Whatever the mood, it was always a reflection of my unique design.

Although a move back to my homeland infused the most gloomy, eerie feelings imaginable, the reality remained that I had a great job to return to. The smartest move so far proved to be my decision to take a leave of absence instead of resigning from my position as an administrative assistant at the University of Illinois.

How bad could it be? Cold winters, no social life, just work, workouts, and home. I silently cried, praying for the strength to bear the life I detested.

Champaign-Urbana was so small. Everybody knew everybody, or so it seemed. Most of the brothas fought it out for the title of drug lord, or got locked up because their efforts failed. Desirable, driven, gainfully employed men were limited to a handful. Overall, the mentality in the single scene was lame, making social connections a constant contest.

Those few brothas worth competing for held on to their crowns tight. If a girl wore an outfit that did not win the male review, their eyes would wonder in search of a new prize. The competition was never about talent or intelligence, but about model make up, in other words, you had to thrive on being a dime piece. The game was all about style, about beauty, about envy, about competition, about bullshit in my book.

The eligible playas seemed to wait around for the young tenderonies to emerge into young adulthood, giving them a whole new slate of contestants to grace the stage, better known as the twin cities. The playettes literally used the vanity game as ammunition in their title hopes. The playas held very few crowning ceremonies. That didn't seem to matter because the average reign without game attached was a year, maybe two, tops.

I had outgrown my days of setting the record straight. My four sisters and I were truly some of the prettiest girls to ever charm the twin cities. I took advantage of being the youngest of five girls. I watched my sisters in action before I was ready to take on the dating game. I had an admiration about each of my sisters, one trait I took from each.

Joyce's total sophistication, glamour, and style made her an absolute feminine. Yolanda possessed boldness, a courage to go after anything her heart desired. Vanessa's confidence and drive made her certain about who she was. Lisa's quiet and shy approach projected a wholesome appeal that won the hearts of friends and family.

I took the sleek sophistication, the boldness, the self confidence, the innocent appeal and mixed those attributes with my own uniqueness. I had a way of displaying myself as secretive with buried treasure. In most cases the secrets would go unrevealed except in the few cases of some family, and the few friends I had carefully chosen to gradually unwrap my present appeal, and observe my many gifts.

I had my own day of validation that sealed my game as one of the tightest when I landed a brief romance with a man sought after by females throughout the country. A man as familiar to Americans as email. Let's just say he played a lot of Russian roulette during his bachelor years, throwing his dick out on the crap table many a night. This is just another place where a roll of those precious jewels landed.

I refused to settle for anything but premium, and I knew the flavor of my game was as good as the best. I just assume not land a runner up title that would leave me waiting in the wings for the victor to lose her crown to circumstance. I'd rather not be given the thrown and live under microscopic paranoia about making a wrong move that could cost me a crown. I had no desire to ever walk that runway again.

No matter what my shortcomings, two weeks from now I would be headed back to Illinois. I had hoped and prayed the possibility of making Florida my new home would bring about a life changing challenge. For me, Florida's obstacle was a bilingual asset I did not possess and had no desire to acquire.

I took advantage of the peaceful moments the wee night hours had presented, and crawled out of bed. I quietly scrambled through my things searching for something to put on as I prepared for a serene moment in the bathtub alone with my thoughts.

The bath bubbles and oils filled the room with a delicious vanilla scent. I lit my vitality candle and turned off the light switch. I slipped my thumbs in the waistband of my baggy gym shorts maneuvering them down my hips letting them drop to the floor.

I stepped into my hot bath and let my body sink in the pool of bubbles. I changed the CD in my portable walkman to a soothing Sade and indulged in a much needed session of meditation. I whispered a silent prayer for the strength to accept my choice to leave.

I wiped my face, and went over my bronze body, giving the small towel a single chance to absorb the beads of water on my shiny skin. My slinky floral sun dress slid down my slender waist, clinging to my shapely hips. My dark brown hair, wet from the bath instantly curled into spirals falling down to the tip of my shoulders. I brushed my teeth and fluffed my hair with my fingers.

I took my cologne out of my make up bag, which was as bold as my personality. Flowery perfumes never fit my persona, it was the boldness of the men's fragrances that best defined my daring nature, and that secret went rarely revealed. My natural body oils defined the scent in my feminine taste. I sprayed it in a circular motion around my body letting it fall like a light sprinkle of rain.

I finished my look with a single silver hoop earring with a cross charm in my right ear, and a small silver ball post in my left, something I had done long before Janet Jackson broke out in it with her pleasure principles. My rare style was as unique as my unmatched earrings, an unsurpassed image that is not only mysterious, I am a bona fide, like a puzzle, a mystery gone very deep.

Dressed for the day I walked in the kitchen and made coffee. The clock on the microwave read four thirty-nine. I sat in deep thought on the living room couch where the faint light of day tried hard to break through the black velour mini blinds. I ran my index finger around the rim of my Precious Moments coffee mug as the steam from the coffee seeped through my fingers.

Suddenly I thought about my best friend Danita Neilson, who I hadn't seen in over six months. She had moved from Champaign to Nashville over a year ago. The thought occurred that I could spend the last two weeks of my leave with her. The fact that Nashville was on the way to Illinois iced the idea. The thought sparked off a new flow of adrenaline. Why not, I thought, I was on vacation.

I quickly traded my glass mug for a taller plastic one, filling it with coffee as I headed out the door. The streets were deserted. The drive through town left the harmonious flashing traffic lights flickering on the hood of my black Mitsubishi Gallant, while the sound of water from the rain under the tires, squished on the pavement.

I pushed number one on my CD changer and set the mood for my own private party featuring Aaliyah. I let her plant the seed of One in a Million. Once on I-4, I let her rest after her four page letter, and let 2Pac break me into day with his prophecy flavor, while I wondered and anticipated what Nashville would be like. My favorite way to unwind was served up right, a ride all alone with my thoughts and music.

The drive down the interstate relaxed me. The sight of beautiful green pastures, and tall city buildings were refreshing and breathed life into me.

As the sun began to heat up the city, a foggy smoke rose above the wet asphalt from the rising heat. The traffic started to build, filling the expressway with Thursday morning commuters piling in from every direction.

The reality of my decision to move back home, settled slowly in my soul. I headed back toward Lakeland to avoid the hectic traffic. I knew there would be no looking back, no turning around. The ten hour drive to Nashville would be my opportunity to contemplate my plan for my return home to the twin cities in two weeks. I headed back to the house to tell my brother and sister-in-law about my plan, and to call Danita.

The quiet house buzzed a ring of silence in my ears. I packed my bags and finished some material I wanted to print, and loaded my computer in the trunk.

My brother was my father's son from his first marriage. He was the big brother I had always wanted growing up. We met when I was eight, and he fell right into his role, and played the part well. His wife Regina was truly an undercover angel. She had a way of reaching distraught souls seeking comfort. I have always loved to sit back and watch her work. They were both disappointed that I was leaving, but supportive of my decision.

I moved some money around in my bank accounts, washed my car, and filled my gas tank. I took off after a long nap at almost two in the morning. It was the time I liked driving the long highways best, in the middle of the night. I loved the night skies, when the only natural light to be found shined by the power of the stars.

# Chapter 2

When Danita opened the door to her brick townhouse we embraced each other. I was greeted by a lopsided portrait of black Jesus, centered on the wall above the fireplace. When my eyes met with those of Jesus I felt an instant energy. I couldn't resist walking over to the wall to align this splendid piece of art.

The room was small and well lit through the valance draped over the window's frame. The sun shined brightly through the white mini blinds. The plain emerald green sofa, and matching love seat, arranged in a sectional style, faced the oak entertainment center filled with family photos. Danita had never been the most creative when it came to home decor, but the warmth and love that filled the room could not to be mistaken.

I have loved being around Danita since we met eight years ago, and I realized how much I had missed her since she left home. Danita had a great sense of humor and loved to laugh. She was what brothas call a thick red bone. Her skin was the color of caramel with a reddish tint. There was nothing fat about her. Her arms, thighs and legs were just thick. Her frame was as close as you could get to hour glass. Her medium length, reddish brown hair was barely curled, framing her round face that showed off the deep dimples buried in her cheeks.

Danita timed a late breakfast almost precise to the minute. The small dining room table was already set. The smell of fresh baked croissants and coffee filled the air. Danita knew I loved me some hot black coffee, and poured me a fresh cup in a tall glass mug.

Danita pulled a dinner plate from the microwave with slices of steaming ham. I put the croissants and cheese on the table. Danita poured herself a tall glass of milk, and piled in three heaping spoons of nestle quick, and stirred it chocolate. We sat across from each other, and made hot ham and cheese croissants.

"So, you really left Champaign?" Danita asked.

"Girl, I just can't believe how different Florida is when you're not on vacation. The best part about the whole trip was meeting this guy who is also a writer. He writes plays," I said.

"So who is this guy? Is he cute?"

"Yes girl, baby is fine. His name is Scott. We met at the gym. He got on the treadmill next to me, and asked what I was listening to through the earplug of my little hand held recorder. That of course, brought about a conversation about my writing, and we learned we had that interest in common," I said. "We learn from each other. He has excellent proofing and criticism skills. He shares his thoughts with me and, I help create his needed conflict. I critique him, he critiques me and we are both gaining. I get a rush from him. He really motivates me."

Scott Marshall really understood and could connect with me. We each valued what we had in common and made the most of it. We had grown into a routine of having lunch together to talk and swap material for the constructive criticism sessions we each used to enhance our work.

Scott kept in touch with me through the voice mail I had gotten instead of my own phone line at my brother's house. Scott was as hard to reach as I was. We constantly played tag until we ended up making a date through voice mails for the live conversation we would have at our next lunch.

"So how is your writing coming along anyway?" Danita asked.

"It has been awesome. I can't tell you the connection I feel I have right now. A sister is flowing. I couldn't be happier with that part of my life," I said. "So how is your nursing going? What are you, a CNT, right?"

"Yes. It's okay, not exactly what I planned on. When I was in school it was exciting. I thought I would want to keep moving up in ranks, but I don't want to go another further. I still have to deal with the drama of superiors and personality conflicts," she said. "But it pays my bills, it pays my telephone bill, it pays my automobile."

"You are so crazy. I want to be a comedian like you when I grow up," I said.

"No you don't. You are the destiny child," she said. "You found writing. Me, I'm still exploring."

Danita's live in man Terry, came down the stairs in a black terry cloth robe that hid his silk pajamas.

"Hey Freeze," I said. "Long time no see."

Terry was upbeat, unique and charming. I met him in Champaign about a year ago when he came to see Danita. He was a rapper, and he really fit the part. His nickname was Freeze, I guess that meant he was as cold as ice. He was tall and slim. He was growing dreads and wore a spaghetti thin beard line and equally thin mustache, and goat-t that framed his oval face. His cocoa skin was smooth and his teeth were perfect, and pearl white. Danita had a thing for a man with a nice grill.

"It's nice to see you again," he said. "Danita has been excited about you coming."

I helped clear the table and load the dishwasher. I was eager to see Nashville, but was beat from the long drive.

"I need a nap," I said. "Where am I sleeping Danita?"

"Where are your bags?" Freeze asked.

"In my car," I said. I handed him the keys. "Most everything I need is in the back seat.

"I'll bring everything in, and take it upstairs for you."

"Thanks," I said.

"Here come on, I'll show you to your room," Danita said. "Right this way madam."

Danita led me upstairs to the second bedroom. I looked around the room that had obviously been used as a catch all. The baby blue walls were bare. The small window was covered by a pair of beige curtains that looked like a burlap sack. A brass daybed was centered along the long wall. The dresser was next to a set up ironing board, and clean laundry was piled in a black recliner waiting to be folded.

I reviewed my self made set of mental tools that I created for the purpose of maintaining my inner peace. I was convinced they could potentially lead me to my destiny. I tried not to ponder the thought they had failed me. I couldn't afford to allow any negative energy to find dwelling inside me. Instead, I kept the faith in the centerness I had found. All that mattered to me was that I truly believed in them with all my heart.

My needed meditation was interrupted by the almost instant sleep that overtook me in just a few moments.

# Chapter 3

Boys in the Hood came to mind when I caught my first real glimpse of Nashville. The roads were laid out like a roller coaster, with sharp curves, and crooked roads. The streets winded around unsightly landscaping. Weeds and unmowed grass made an eye sore. The view from a hill top was an attractive sight, especially at night fall, but it wasn't as pleasant as a ride through greater Orlando. Pot holes, and uneven pavement on the roads was another of its homely characteristics. When they say the dirty south, they mean it, literally.

Nashville was of a different culture, a different feeling. There was no south of the border look everywhere you turned, no groups engaged in conversation I didn't understand. Instead it was a taste of chocolate mocha served up at its best, especially in the area where Danita lived on the north side.

Almost immediately, I become aware of the friendly nature. The Nashvillians always had a warm smile, a wave, or a friendly hello. It was refreshing compared to a cold Illinois where it was taboo to speak to strangers. Oh my goodness, and the brothas, they were everywhere, a fine mixture of any flavor imaginable. Tiny beads of sweat formed on my forehead from the shock of seeing so many brothas in one place.

Danita showed me the way to the car wash on Ewing Lane. A small barber shop called Hair Designs was directly across the street next to a Baskin Robbins. I watched brotha after brotha coming and going from there.

"Ah," I said as I took in a deep breath of relief. "That is a trip. Baskin Robbins is packed with flavors, but they can't touch what's going on next door. The real flavor is at the barber shop."

"Girl, this is not the half of it," Danita said.

The amount of brothas gave a broad range of class and style to choose from. Most were classic country, and groomed themselves accordingly.

"I get the impression they think gold teeth are a good thing, an attractive accessory." I said. "That would be a negative my brothas."

That night we went to a club called Yesterday's. A large, two tier dance floor was the center of attention. They balanced the atmosphere with a chilled area where tables were set up with tall studio chairs. The bar sat smack dab in the middle.

We found a table near the dance floor. I ordered hot wings from the small kitchen in the back, and a gin and tonic. Danita had a vodka and orange juice. There were four pool tables in along the far side wall where the second bar extended around to the DJ booth. The mirrored walls made the club look larger than it was.

My first taste of the Nashville night life was filled with a buffet of brothas. So many that I wasn't sure what my taste buds were feeling. I met a lot of people who weren't originally from the state. You could almost tell instantly, and with a sense of certainly, which ones they were. A nice photographer named Arnez was set up in a corner selling club pictures with the famous felt backgrounds. He took our picture to commemorate the moment.

Several polite, handsome men approached us, and we lost our table after spending so much time on the dance floor. We decided to wait for a pool table, and played a few rounds before calling it a night.

"I have an extra bedroom and I could use a roommate Michelle," Danita said. "Why don't you stay here?"

"I don't even have to think twice, but what about Freeze?"

"Me and Freeze are having some issues anyway," Danita said. "My name is on the lease, not ours. You are my best friend. If he doesn't like it he can walk."

"I don't want to come between your relationship. I'd feel better if you talked to him about it first."

"Okay, I'll talk to him," she said. "So is that a yes?"

"Yes, it's a yes."

A few days later, I could tell Danita had talked to Freeze by his behavior. Although he tried to hide it, there was no mistake. I could tell he had some issues with me, I just didn't know the specifics. All I could guess was that he felt invaded. Danita had been with me the entire time I had been there when she wasn't working. He worked second shift at a local prison so I rarely saw him.

I made the decision to make some good on my commitment to go back to Illinois. I decided I would stay long enough to prepare a training manual for my replacement, since I had given my boss the hope that I would be back to stay.

Danita and I were having the time of our lives catching up on the time we had been separated and all that had happened. We were never without words, and conversation flowed every minute we were together. Days were peaceful, and the nights were exciting and lively.

When the day started to approach for me to go fulfill my obligation, I realized how quickly the two weeks in the 'Ville had rolled by. I wished that I had detoured to Nashville nine weeks ago. By now I could have landed a decent job, and could be living the life I had dreamed of for so long.

# Chapter 4

I awoke to the buzzing alarm clock, and reached without looking to find the snooze button. I squinted my eyes, to keep from being blinded by the bright red digital numbers. Normally I opened my eyes without hesitation, but the night of sleep had been filled with some intense dreams I could not ignore. My dream world was in such a full swing that once recorded, many of them left my mind once the pen had inked the event.

I headed out of Nashville about three in the morning. The sights on the highway went from hills and mountains to flat farm land. My mood changed with the scenery. At the halfway point of the six hour drive home, I crossed over the bridge that separated Kentucky and Illinois. I rolled my eyes at the sign that welcomed me.

The change was extreme. The traffic moved at a slower pace to stay within the reduced speed limit, turning my mood to a lower tempo like a fireplace log losing it's flame. I dreaded the two weeks, and I couldn't wait to get back home. Danita and I had planned to meet up in Florida to retrieve my belongings to move to Nashville.

The time in Illinois brought to light the coldness of the Midwest nature that drove me away. The weather was up and down like a yo-yo. The slow moving traffic on the city streets was tiring and made the days long. The highway was not expressed, there are only four Champaign, Urbana exits that all lead nowhere.

I knew I didn't belong there. My final destination may not be Nashville, but I know my direction will never lead me to this camp again.

The mentality was as lame as it was when I left. When I got caught up on the gossip and news from the last nine weeks, I learned of even more people in the death trap of the twin cities who had bitten the dust. Champaign was turning into a replica of Waco, Texas. People everywhere were allowing themselves to get burned up. The crack was rising in popularity and fame like a celebrity, and was literally running the streets. I knew I had made the right choice when I decided to leave.

The walls in the hallways at work were closing in on me during my first hours back. I received a warm welcome, but found my old desk in a disarray. The interim assistant had baskets everywhere to keep up with the various demands of the warehouse operation. My boss must have read the depression in my eyes. He sent me to the computer center, where I checked out a laptop to compile the data for my manual away from the office.

I eagerly made my way to my friend LaTasha's house, a former coworker who kept herself and her life as secretive as an undercover spy. At her place I didn't have to worry about anyone distracting me from the mission I was out to accomplish.

I opened the vertical blinds that covered the big picture window that framed her charming patio. The sun shined in on her impressive condo that was decorated with such good taste, it was like walking around in the pages of a magazine of modern interior. The cozy atmosphere made it easy for me to work quickly. Her place was a great escape from the drama and harsh realities that filled the streets outside.

The bright sun casted a blurry shadow over the big screen television that I kept on to listen to CNN to keep up on world events. During the day I was there alone while she worked. I kept pecking away, typing every requirement it took to make the busy office run as smooth as silk. I deleted the drama going on outside from my mind and put together a manual I was proud to leave with Bob.

When the day to leave Illinois finally came I was exhausted. I thought August 9 would never come. I felt like I had served a short prison sentence. I breathed in a breath of the dull airplane air and gazed out the window from my coach seat on the 747. I lost myself in my thoughts as I looked at the fluffy white clouds that filled the sky. I knew that Danita and I had our work cut out for us. If everything went as planned, we would be back on the road to Tennessee in 24 hours. I blew out a long sigh of anguish at the thought of the work to come.

My daydream was interrupted by the pilot, whose voice played over the intercom system. "Good evening passengers. We are 95 miles northeast of our destination. The weather is warm and the skies are breezy in St. Petersburg with a current temperature of 82 degrees. The flight attendants will be preparing us to land. Thank you, and I hope you had a pleasant flight."

When I merged from the chute, I came out of my white wind breaker, and stuffed it in my duffel bag. All I could hear was the swish from my white jogging pants that sounded like sandpaper with each of my long strides. I followed the signs to find the car rental counter where the agent was standing working a newspaper crossword puzzle.

After signing my rental agreement I wrote down the directions for a shortcut to the interstate. I made my way out to the parking lot where the smell of salty ocean water blew in the wind. I looked at my watch and estimated arriving at the Orlando International Airport about twenty minutes after Danita's flight was scheduled to land.

# Chapter 5

The spirit of Kirk Neilson stood with his arms resting over the top of the passenger side of the blue Ford Taurus waiting for Michelle.

"Hi Michelle, I'm Kirk Neilson, Danita's father," he said.

"Hi Kirk, it's nice to meet you," Michelle's voice spoke. Like Kirk, her lips were not moving. It was her unconscious talking back to him, "I'm on my way to pick Danita up from the airport in Orlando," she said.

"I'm here on business," he said. "And I have a good feeling you are going to be easy to work with,"

"Work?" She asked. "I sir, am officially unemployed."

Kirk's spirit slid in the passenger seat through the closed door. Michelle climbed in and threw her duffel bag in the back seat. She tuned in the radio station and started to sing.

"I met your mother," he said. "We're working together to appeal a case that involves you and your dream to write."

Her unconscious spoke back. "Writing is my passion, but you obviously know that."

Michelle merged into traffic on the secondary street in St. Petersburg.

"Danita and I are best friends," she said.

"You happen to be more than best friends. Danita stands to learn a lot from you. The thing I came to tell you is, that in order for our work to pay off, I have to take your recent dreams temporarily out of your conscious, so that you don't lose focus."

"Okay Boss, if you say so," her unconscious said. "Since I don't know anything about what you do, I'll leave the specifics up to you."

"Well since you just named me boss, I guess I should tell you I'm going to have to put some obstacles in your way," Kirk laughed.

"Gee thanks, I guess it's nice that you're telling me."

Michelle's conscious was singing a tune on the radio. She flipped on the dome lamp and read the directions she held in her hand to find the interstate.

"I have to close the door between your subconscious and your conscious," Kirk said. "All you have to do is utilize those tools you have on your burner."

"If you know me, then you know I try to keep my channel locked, and staying tuned is tool number seven."

"Yes, but are you really practicing the same thing you try and preach?"

"I think so."

Tiny drops of rain accumulated and quickly dried, leaving spots on the layer of dust that had collected on the windshield. The airport traffic in Orlando was busy. Michelle got behind a shuttle bus that slowed her paced speed. She rounded the exit ramp and pulled up to the passenger pick up area where Danita was supposed to meet her. She pulled behind a black taxi, turned on the emergency blinkers, and headed toward the airport entrance looking through the crowd outside trying to spot Danita.

Kirk's transparent form plowed through the crowd of

commuters as he slowly approached a concrete bench where Danita was lying on her back. His trench coat hung on his glassy form, and his hands were hidden in the pockets. Danita's head was propped on her duffel bag with her arms folded over her head.

"Hi baby," Kirk said.

Danita moved her arms from over her face and appeared to be looking at her father. Her tired eyes, were bloody red. She sat up and regained her focus while swift moving travelers passed her by. Minus lip movement, she responded. "Hi daddy. How have you been?"

"Fine honey," Kirk said.

"I can't get over how good you look. Why are you here?"

"I'm here to let you know that you will be working with Michelle on a project. I want you to stay close to her and absorb her philosophies."

"Why daddy?"

"I know how much you want to be married. I want you to be patient and wait for your husband to reveal himself. I don't want you to end up with the wrong person just for the sake of saying I do. I want you to use this time you have with Michelle to grow and learn some things about your inner spirit."

Danita looked at her watch, and fluffed her hair with her thick fingers.

"Michelle is waiting for you," Kirk said. He pointed to Michelle who was describing Danita to a woman placing her baby in a stroller. The lady shook her head indicating she had not seen the woman Michelle was describing. Just then, Michelle turned and spotted Danita.

"Bye Daddy, it was good to see you," her unconscious

said. Danita gazed at her father with loving eyes.

Kirk turned away and pushed right through the big picture window of the airport, and disappeared in the busy crowd.

# Chapter 6

I cupped my hands together, making them into a makeshift bullhorn. "Danita," I yelled.

"Hey girl. I had fallen asleep on a bench," Danita said. She ran over to me and we headed for the rental car.

"How was your flight?" I asked. I unlocked the car doors.

"Good, how was yours?"

"It was okay, I get lost on airplanes, I hated it had to end." I dug in my purse and positioned the mirror to touch up my copper colored lipstick. I picked some coins out of my change bag that hung on the inside of my small brown handbag.

"It makes me sleepy, but I'm juiced now. Let's go out tonight. Thursday has to be ladies night somewhere in Florida."

"Are you sure you feel like it? Your eyes are rose red."

"I just woke up," she said. "There is no way I'm going to come all this way and not get a taste of the night life. That's why we came prepared."

I slowed down just enough to throw my money in the toll basket, and eased the car up until the gate lifted, and the light turned green. When we got closer to Kissimmee, the bright lights radiated a magical appeal over the sky. Danita gazed around carefully, enjoying her first look at Florida.

"Well, it is as pretty as I had imagined it would be," she said.

"This area is especially nice. There is a time every night when you can ride through here and watch the fireworks they do at Disney."

It was almost eleven when I merged onto I-4. I set the cruise on seventy two, a speed that kept pace with the hurried traffic on the busy interstate. A dark green Acura, an upgrade from ghetto-mobiles, with sparkly rims, pulled up beside us. Danita rolled down her window.

The hunk of chocolate in the car next to us leaned over to look at Danita. He worked a cool number that landed his chin in the palm of his hand. His fingers explored his cheeks for hair that wasn't there.

"Hey, what's going on?" Danita asked. She tried to scope out all the passengers with one scan. The driver was a dark chocolate brotha with jet black curly hair. His face was as clean as a baby's bottom, with not a stitch of facial hair. The man in the passenger seat wore a bald fade, and a thin mustache. His skin was almost yellow, and a toothpick danced around in his mouth.

"What's going on Baby?"

"My name is Danita," she said. Danita hated to be called any term of endearment by strangers. "What's yours?"

"Clinton."

"Where is the party?"

"Do you know where Hero's is?"

Danita turned to me. I nodded yes to the beat of my song that played on the radio in the background. Chill bumps collected on my arms from the gripping night air. I slowly turned the volume back up while trying to keep pace with the man in the Acura.

"She knows where it is."

"Yall going?" Clinton said.

"Yeah, we'll be there."

I used that as my queue to break the road dance. I sped up just enough to pass in front of another car to lose the Acura.

"We have to change clothes," Danita said. "Let's go to your brother's house."

"No way, that's 40 miles the other way," I said.

"Well stop at a restaurant."

"That's roguish."

"So what? Are you funky?" Danita said. She did a smell check under her arms. "I'm good. Are you good? We've only flown, it's not like we hitched our way here in the heat."

When we exited in Winter Park, I pulled in a parking space at Denny's next to a red Prelude shaking my head about our ghetto fabulous plan.

"Okay, let's put everything we need in one bag," Danita said. "I'll carry it in."

"This is weird," I said.

"This is free," Danita said laughing.

I felt funny about not buying anything. Danita didn't even offer the employees a look, she headed straight for the rest room. When I walked in behind her, she had already plugged in her curling iron.

"You are so bold," I said. "I bet they think we're hookers. Damn, how embarrassing."

"But, I'm going to be cute though."

I went in the handicap stall and slipped into my short, slinky green dress. I came out and slid my bare feet in my black pumps.

"That dress is so cute. You're just glittering everywhere, all up in Denny's where you're not buying a damn thing," Danita laughed.

"That's it. You take as long as you need. I will put on my make-up and do my hair in the car."

Danita clipped the hot irons in my direction. "Sure you don't want a curl or two?"

"Don't worry about me, just take your time sister," I said. "Holla."

I had to ignore the nosy eyes that watched me on my way back to the car. They probably thought we were a couple of street walkers looking for a free place to freshen up. I couldn't believe I let Danita talk me into this. I held my head down and didn't feel any relief until I positioned the rearview mirror on my innocent face. I felt paranoid and kept thinking some weirdo would come up and knock on the window and make me an offer.

I touched up my makeup, and brushed my hair up into a sophisticated French roll to compliment my elegant mini dress. Danita walked out of Denny's a few minutes later. She made it worse when she switched her ghetto ass fiercely, giggling as she headed to the car.

# Chapter 7

Strobe lights flooded the big dance floor that was covered by big squares of black and white linoleum in a checkerboard design. The lights danced in rhythm to the slightly loud music. Large pillars reached the high ceiling and were scattered to support the building's old structure. The walls were painted glossy black, and small mismatched tables surrounded by black banquet chairs were arranged in all four corners. A long bar extended halfway across one wall where black bar stools lined its frame.

Clinton was standing at the bar and motioned for us to join him. He and his friend Tommy bought a round of drinks and we all got aquatinted.

The smell of stale beer filled the dry air. The crowd was more relaxed in their culture than we were used to. A lot of blue jeans and short outfits were the attire of choice, a flavor very different from the Midwest, and even Nashville.

"One of us would have won a best dressed contest in a heartbeat," Danita said.

"Hands down," Clinton said. "Yall got it going on."

"You can shole tell we ain't from round hear," Danita said speaking with an exaggerated country accent.

"I feel the same vibe 2Pac did, all eyes on me. I feel the stares of what seems to be a million pairs of eyes looking hard, but they don't realize that they'll never see me," I said.

Danita and Clinton laughed. Tommy just shook his head. He had been so busy looking me up and down that I suppose he knew I was talking about him too.

Clinton and Tommy were greeted by another brotha. They all shared the handshake, giving each other five sideways and flipping their fingers and making their hands dance together. The newcomer looked at me and Danita. He gave the backwards nod to acknowledge us. I turned and scanned the room, and spotted a man whose eyes felt glued to me.

"I hate that," I said.

"What?" Danita asked.

"When men stare. Check out how this brotha, he has no shame. You would think he would try and keep it low-key and turn his head when I look his way," I said.

This tall hunk of a man was posted up near the dance floor. He was leaned on a pillar with his long legs spread apart holding a drink in his hand. His attire was either black or a very dark blue. He looked very tall, and broad across the shoulders.

When Danita went to dance with Clinton, I turned around on the barstool, crossed my bold bare legs with grace and ordered another drink. When the bartender set the drink in front of me on a napkin, an arm reached over my shoulder holding a twenty dollar bill. I turned to find the tall man who I had only seen in silhouette standing over me.

"Let me get a Heineken," he said. "Mind if I buy your drink?"

"That's nice, but it's already been paid for," I said. "Thank you though." I had two drinks bought for me by admirers somewhere in the club. I wasn't ready at the time, but the bartender was keeping track of my credit.

The man standing over me offered his hand to me. I placed my hand in his with a delicate touch. "Hi, my name is Michelle Cooper."

"It's nice to meet you Michelle. My name is Ricky Howell," he said. "Do you live here?"

"Well I spent seven weeks hoping to make a life here, but I changed my mind."

"You don't like Florida?" he asked.

"It's okay. It is a lot more fun to do on vacation. I'm originally from Illinois, so the culture here is very different," I said. "I'm here to get my things out of storage. I've decided to move to Nashville."

"So what's wrong with Florida?"

"If I had to narrow it down to a single thing, I'd say the bilingual factor."

"So what do you do?"

"I've worked in administration for the last five years to pay the bills, but I'm a writer in my spare time. I had hoped to get some of my plays on stage out here, but I would've had to pay the bills too you know," I said. "What about you?"

"I'm a math teacher, sixth grade," he said. "How long are you here for?"

"I'm out of here sometime tomorrow afternoon."

Ricky was tall, dark and built. His oval face was scarred with lines of stitch marks. He shared with me how he had been involved in a car accident that nearly cost him his life. The scars were hardly enough to take away from his attractiveness. Like me, he loved to laugh and we cracked many jokes.

We talked and danced until the lights in the club came on

for last call. Danita had pulled a disappearing act, and finally reappeared. Her face was drained from dancing. She plopped down on the bar stool next to me, ordered an ice water and fanned her face with her hands. She sat panting like she had just run a relay.

"Who's this?" she asked.

"This is Ricky Howell," I said. "Ricky, this is my best friend, Danita Neilson."

Danita introduced me to a Jamaican guy she had met. Steve's round face was hidden behind his long dread locks. His blue striped shirt hung over his baggy jeans. He seemed kind of raggedy but the look worked for him.

Outside the night air barely blew a breeze. The crowd was slowly thinning out. Danita and her friend walked close behind me and Ricky on our way to the car. The parking lot was dimly lit, and several groups of people were engaged in small talk. Ricky wrote his phone number in my address book.

"Where are you headed?" he asked.

"We were planning on going to my brother's house. But I think we might play it safe and get a room on the other side of Kissimmee since we've been drinking. I don't want to be far from Lakeland, that's where I'm picking the truck up from tomorrow."

"I live in Altamonte Springs. You two can crash at my place if you want to."

"No thanks. I think we'll stick to our plan," I said, "My storage space is in Altamonte Springs though. How about I call you after we get there?"

"Call me when you get settled in your room," he said.

Steve offered to pay for our room, and Danita accepted

providing there were no strings attached. I followed Steve and Danita in his rented convertible to the hotel and waited for him to check us in. He offered to buy breakfast and we went across the street to Denny's. I refused to be a third wheel, and ordered my breakfast to go so Danita and Steve could dine alone.

I made my way inside the spacious room with two double beds. It reeked of chlorine from the huge swimming pool outside. I looked at the clock and decided to try and call Ricky even though it was well past three.

"Are you still awake?" I asked.

"What took so long?" he asked, "I was beginning to worry."

"We went for breakfast after we checked in."

"Are you sure I can't persuade you to come over tonight? I'll come and get you and take you back in the morning."

"No, but thanks," I said. "I have to get some sleep. We have a long drive ahead of us. I'll call you tomorrow."

When the phone rang with the scheduled wake up call, I forced my eyes open long enough to look at the time. It felt like I had just rested my head on the pillow. I looked over at the other bed to make sure Danita made it in. I drug myself out of bed and into the bathroom where I started a cool shower. When I came out Danita was still struggling to get out of bed.

"We need to get a move on Danita," I said. "I'm going to the lobby for coffee, do you want some?"

"Yes," Danita said in a groggy, sleepy voice. "Put about three sugars and a cream in it. If they have some danish or something, get me one of those too."

I came back to the room out of the rising heat where the

sound of the shower sounded like a rush of heavy rain. I bit into the apple danish and sipped my hot black coffee. I sat at the small table in front of the window and opened the drapes slightly. I thought about this being the last time I would see Florida for a while. I dreaded the long drive to Nashville. Loading the truck was going to be murder in the intense midday heat. I prayed until Danita broke my moment when she shut off the shower.

# Chapter 8

It was just after ten when we pulled into the lot of the U-Haul dealer. The ten foot truck I had reserved did not appear to be among those in the lot. I dug the reservation confirmation out of my purse and went inside to see what was going on.

"Mam we are very sorry," the clerk said. "Your truck was scheduled to be returned to us last night but the renter never showed up."

"What am I supposed to do about that?" I asked.

"If you'd like, you can have a twenty four foot truck for the same price, or I can have my husband pick up a truck from another location."

"I don't want to drive a twenty four foot truck for ten hours. Go ahead and have him get a truck. I'll give you my brother's phone number, and you can call me when it's ready. I hope that won't take too long." I tried to be understanding, but I'm sure my attitude was showing through my phony smile.

An hour later, I signed the contract for the truck. We pulled off the lot and I couldn't believe there was something wrong with it.

"Oh hell no," I said. "I can't believe this."

Pushing the accelerator all the way to the floor couldn't make the truck go faster than thirty miles an hour. I turned around and went back to the dealer. After a quick inspection of the truck, the agent found a transmission problem. I was furious.

While I waited for my credit card to be voided I called the

rental car company and arranged to drop the car off in Nashville.

"I still have to get some stuff out of my storage space. I'm not sure how much we can fit in the car, but we'll have to do the best we can. I am trying to find the blessing here. At least I'm not moving from one storage space to another, besides, my brother got me hooked up for a deal with the space I have now."

The fast moving traffic on I-4 coupled with the sun shiny weather gave me the rush that had hooked me to Florida in the first place.

We felt the impact of the intense heat as we rummaged through the boxes in my storage space. I came across some place mats and tossed one to Danita. We stood at the door fanning ourselves. We were desperate for some wind in the dry heat. Our tanning skin was tinted red, and flushed from the sun.

Danita leaned back on the wall and slid her body down to a stooped position. "I'm dying over here," she said. "I had no idea the sun could be so hot."

"I think I have most everything I need," I said. "My work clothes and shoes are the most important."

After piling everything that would fit in the trunk and back seat I locked up the unit. It was so hot, that I left the place disorderly instead of taking the time to tidy it up. We sat in the car and let the cool air fill the inside. Finally we drove around the corner to a convenience store for a cold drink.

"I guess I'll call Ricky," I said.

"Oh hell no. Stop the presses, stop the damn presses," Danita said. "You, follow up with a man you met at a club? Girl this heat has you tripping."

"Being around you is like drinking a cup of courage," I

said. "I get bolder when I have my partner in crime by my side."

"Don't put it off on me if he turns out to be psycho. You know how men get about you, craaazy, and deraaanged. Don't have him flying to Nashville, coming up in Yesterday's in his footies talking about, why you always got to be going to the club?" She said laughing, while doing her famous impression of Martin Lawrence.

# Chapter 9

I was familiar enough with Orlando that I had no problem finding the upscale community. The two toned, white, and sky blue buildings were widely separated over a couple of acres. Big palm trees were scattered around tiny lakes and streams. The scenic grounds made ideal, thought provoking places for relaxation. The air was filled with the smell of fresh flowers that were carefully planted in the landscaping. Automatic sprinklers kept the grass a true green. Two swimming pools sparkled like shining glass in the bright sun. The screened in balcony unit was on the third floor.

"Come in," Ricky called out from the other side of the door.

"Hey Ricky," I said. I didn't remember exactly what he looked like, but the man who's first impression to my eye was in silhouette, struck me again as a hunk of tasty chocolate.

Ricky was sitting on the sofa in a pair of gym shorts, and a muscle T-shirt. His left hand was cupped behind his shiny bald head, and the remote to the TV in the palm of his other hand. His leg was propped on the coffee table. His milk chocolate skin was smooth, except for his scars that appeared more visible in the light.

My flavor filled variety showed through my drastic change in attire from the night before. Ricky's eyes lit up when he saw me. I knew my curvy frame was on point. He looked at me as if it was the first time he had laid eyes on me.

My bold spandex short body suit, with colors scattered like puzzle pieces, gripped my thick smooth thighs. My booty was banging, fit and firm from working out. My arms and legs displayed an athletic tone. I wore a baseball cap with my long ponytail pulled through the opening in the back, and my single silver hoop hung in my right ear.

The air smelled of carpet fresh. The apartment was neatly decorated and impressively clean for a young man. An eggshell, leather sectional sofa lined the wall in front of the big picture window that was covered with cream colored, open drapes. The sun's rays shined on the kitchen, breakfast nook and dining area that were all in open view. The place lacked a woman's touch. The walls were bare, and tall stacks of magazines were piled under the glass coffee table.

Danita asked to use the rest room and I shared the drama of the day with Ricky. I walked over to the large black entertainment center to admire the pictures that lined the shelves while I waited my turn to freshen up. I gave Ricky the eye candy he was asking for when I felt his eyes glued to me.

"Since you don't have a moving truck to worry about, why don't you stay another night and leave in the morning?" Ricky asked.

"I'm really not trying to pay for this car another day," I said.

"I'll pay for the extra day," Ricky said. "Stay and come to my game."

"What kind of game?" I asked.

"Football."

"Football in August?" I asked. "I thought you were a

teacher?"

"I am. I also play for the arena league. I have to be there at six, but the game doesn't start until seven. I have some tickets in my truck."

"Come on Michelle," Danita said, as she stopped to admire the pictures. "It'll be fun."

"Okay, but we need to get something to eat," I said, "I'll need to get something to wear, all I have are sweats and a T-shirt besides my work wardrobe in the car."

"You look fine the way you are," Ricky said.

"Um, I've been sweating to death in the sun all day. I could use a shower and a fresh look."

"Cool," Ricky said. "There's a key in the gym shoe on the balcony so you can get back in. The linen closet is right next to the bathroom. Walk down with me and I'll get you the tickets. Do you know where the arena is?"

"Yes, it's where the Magic play right?" I asked.

"Yeah, that's it," he said.

As soon as I accepted the invitation to the game, it seemed to give Ricky a new adrenaline rush. His voice went from nonchalant, to verbal excitement. It was about fifteen minutes before five, so I guess he had hoped and waited for me to call all day.

Ricky stepped inside his bedroom and came out wearing blue jeans and a team T-shirt. He had a black gym bag and gym shoes in his hands. When we walked out the door, sure enough, there was a lonely gym shoe on the balcony.

I had never heard of arena football, but was up for some

fun and excitement. Ricky got two tickets out of the glove compartment of his green Rodeo and handed them to me. He gave me an innocent peck on the lips.

"I'll see you after the game," he said.

We all left at the same time. Ricky headed in the direction to the rear of the complex. Danita and I headed out and went to TJMaxx. We stopped at Popeye's for chicken before going back to Ricky's to eat and shower, before heading to the game.

The traffic jam on I-4 was like a five o'clock rush hour.

"What the heck is this?" I asked.

The closer we got to the arena, we realized the intensified traffic consisted of fans of the league. After paying six dollars to park, we had to fight the crowd and stand in line for a while before finally getting to our assigned seats.

Based on some of the conversation in our section, we realized we were among the family and friends of the other players. Ricky's friend Reggie came and sat next to us, and introduced himself.

"Hi ladies," he said. "My name is Reggie."

"Hey Reggie," Danita said. "I'm Danita and this is Michelle."

Reggie was a tall toast colored brotha with a round face and big ears. He had a neatly trimmed mustache, and wore a black baseball cap that matched his black and red sweat suit.

Reggie explained the mechanics of arena football and pointed Ricky out on the field. We had a couple of beers and cheered with the crowd. When the victory game ended, Reggie escorted us near an area where tight security guarded all entries to the locker room.

Ricky walked over to the wall. The pads made him look even more built. His booty resembled my own a few hours ago, fit and meaty. He took off his helmet and winked at me. Like most football players, the body was an eyeful. He leaned over to the security guard to clear us to come down.

"I'll meet you all in the hallway after I shower," Ricky yelled up from below.

Reggie was a character full of jokes and kept us entertained while we waited. Ricky finally emerged from the locker room after a host of other players. He wore a pair of black slacks, a black silk dress shirt, and black loafers with no socks. He was wiping the mixture of sweat and water from his face and chest with the white towel that hung over his shoulder. Ricky stopped to sign a little boy's football before he joined us.

Ricky's eyes seemed to light up again when he found me in a sexy brown sun dress that complimented my half exposed thick, golden meaty thighs. He finally got a sight of the glamorous side of me. I wore my hair down and it bounced to all movement with fierce body. He cupped the back of my head with his large hand and kissed my cheek.

We headed down the long corridor. Ricky and I walked with our arms around one another to the exit where mostly female fans stood outside waiting to catch a glimpse of the Predators.

"This is a surprisingly popular sport," I said. "I had never heard of arena football before tonight."

"Yeah they are really into it. Nashville has a team, the Kats," Ricky said. "All I want is to win a bowl game, and go to a professional team in the NFL."

"That sounds like a serious plan," Danita said.

"Rick was actually drafted by a pro team, but his hopes for that were halted by the injuries he suffered in a car accident," Reggie said.

"Yeah, not to mention I had a shady agent," Ricky said. "I go to pro camps every chance I get. I know I have the talent to play in the NFL, it's just a matter of time."

The night air was smooth and slightly cool as it blew like a soft breath on our skin during the short walk to the parking lot.

We all piled in Ricky's truck and he drove to the rental car. Danita and Reggie got out and followed us to a post game party at Chester's in the heart of downtown. The line to get inside made its way around the downtown corner of the small bar and grill.

Ricky used his credentials to bypass the waiting crowd and led us to the VIP section set up outside on a patio where we all enjoyed some drinks. I encouraged Ricky to mingle in the crowd after we were stopped every few seconds by someone wanting a word with him.

"I'll be okay," I said. "Go do your thing."

Danita and I mingled in the crowd. Danita was flirting among the many fine brothas, and there were plenty to choose from. I kept catching Ricky's eye on me, and when our eyes would meet, I gave him a wink and an innocent smile. After Ricky's hour long appearance, we left to get a bite to eat.

"You are something else," Ricky said. He lifted my hand off my lap and cupped his fingers between mine.

"What is that supposed to mean?" I asked.

"I can't explain it, but you have a glow of some kind,"

Ricky said. "It's captivating.

"Thanks," I said. "I think."

"It is definitely a compliment."

Ricky caressed my hand and kissed it softly. We pulled into Applebee's and waited for Danita and Reggie to park. We went in for a late dinner and more drinks before leaving the restaurant. On the way to Ricky's apartment, he pulled into a gas station.

"I want to get some munchies and beer to wind the evening down," he said. "Do you want anything special?"

"No thanks."

He stuck his bald head in the open window with his hands cupped on the frame. "Last chance."

"How about a Payday?" I asked.

"You got it."

Reggie pulled the rental car in the space next to Ricky and went inside. Danita rolled her window down.

"He's reeling you in Michelle," Danita said.

"Yeah right," I said.

"Girl you know your body needs some. Damn what are you waiting for? Ten years is a long time to go without some."

"Two and a half, thank you very much. Okay, so he's fine, so his cologne is hypnotizing, so he's single, and well, he does have a nice body, but we don't know each other. Besides, you talk about me, is Reggie spending the night too?"

"No, actually he lives in the same complex as Ricky," Danita said. "Girl you know I got some digits. I'm going to make a few phone calls."

"It was a lot on the menu at the bar," I said. "How many numbers did you get anyway?"

"It was too many to place an order on the spot," Danita said. "Look at Ricky. He's is in there right now telling Reggie what all he plans to do to you."

"He can't make plans without my consent."

Ricky's apartment quickly came to life when he turned on the stereo. He turned the dimmer down on his pole lamp. Shortly after we came in the door, the phone rang.

"That was my friend Darryl," Ricky said. "He lives in Palm Bay, and he went out here tonight. He's going to crash here, I hope you don't mind that Danita."

"No, this is your place," she said. "Is he single?"

"Yes, he's single. You can sleep in that bedroom, my roommate is out of town. Darryl can crash on the sofa," Ricky said.

By now I knew I had dug myself into a hole. The question was, did I want to get out? It was obvious the plan was for me to share his bedroom.

It had been a long time since I had been romanced, and maybe I could just get me some. It's not like I have man, and apparently Ricky doesn't have a woman. If it happens, I guess it will, I thought.

# Chapter 10

Ricky's bedroom was inviting. His king size, motionless waterbed was made up hotel style. His black, green and red pillows lined the headboard and the comforter wore the same colors in a striped pattern. The master bath was decorated with the same colors and was a perfect match.

I heard Darryl come in. Ricky introduced him to Danita.

"Danita if you need anything, more blankets, they're in here, and help yourself to anything. Make yourself at home," he said. "Peace."

Ricky was still holding up two fingers when he walked in closing the door behind him. His six foot, four inch, 265 pound frame was a sight for wanting eyes.

I had stepped out of my sandals and sat picture posed on the bed. If there was one thing I did well, it was feeding candy to the eye. My legs were together leaned slightly to one side with one raised above the other. I was propped on the pillows allowing my elbows to hold me up. Ricky stood looking at the glamour shot in awe while he unbuttoned his shirt.

"I wish we had met earlier in the summer," he said. "You are so gorgeous."

"Thank you for thinking so, but what does that have to do with anything?"

"Nothing really, but you know the captivation thing I mentioned?" he asked. "Reggie noticed it too."

Ricky let his slacks drop to the floor, and revealed his silk black boxer shorts. His body was chiseled near perfection. He curled his leg under and slid his body close to me, allowing his weight to lay me on my back. My head sank into the fluffy pillows. I stroked his bald head with my fingers, while he explored my body with his large hands.

As gently as his urge would allow him, he began kissing me as he slid my dress over my head. His eyes lit up as when he gazed at my hourglass body that wore a matching bra and g-strings, the same chocolate brown color as my short sun dress. He savored the moment and enjoyed the sight before him. He explored my body with a tender touch, kissing only the exposed parts of my body tenderly.

I rolled on my stomach and raised my ass that melted in Ricky's hands like putty. While he massaged my buttocks, I felt his manhood that was growing in desperate need. He watched me caress my own body while he used his hands to keep up with my grinding rhythm.

He pulled my g-strings aside and tasted my sweet juices. My excited response encouraged him to devour the dripping juice until he captured the drop that ended in an eager explosion. The built up tension had taken refuge, and had been on hold like an Army reserve.

I looked around at him while he gave his manhood a few anxious beats to the sound of my eager orgasm. He turned me over and took off my bra. He reached for a condom in the night stand while I slid out of my own panties. He couldn't wait any longer to feel himself inside me and neither could I. He gave me all he had, holding me tight with his strong arms. I wasn't afraid to touch my own body, and Ricky watched with an intense eye. For the third round I asked to ride him.

"I don't have another condom," he said.

"I can't believe this. If there ever was a time I wanted to take ride it is right now," I said. "Well, I'm not protected."

"I've been fixed." he said.

"You've been fixed?" I asked. "Why?"

"I didn't want to get trapped by anyone. So what do you say?"

"I say I can't believe I'm saying this, but I've got to finish this."

I gave him a night to remember. One thing I could do, although I didn't do it often was to perform like a porn star. I served him a big helping of some good ass pussy. I cut my caged cat loose and let it run wild. I rode him with confidence and aggression until we both moaned in ecstasy.

We laid together with our foreheads touching.

"I've abstained from this for two and a half years," I said.

"Yeah right!"

"Well two years and two months to be exact," I said. "Intimacy is sharing more of me than I usually allow."

"I'm not trying to do no one night stand so I guess you just started something you will have to finish. You are welcome here any time you want. As a matter of fact, if you changed your mind and wanted to stay in Florida, you could live here with me."

"So, you are giving me a green light?"

"I am."

"I can't believe I actually did this after all this time."

"So why did you?"

I gave his question some thought, maybe it was the liquor,

maybe I was just that buzzed, or maybe I was out of control. I knew neither was the case. I was horny, human and I needed some flesh. Being good to me didn't provide the warmth and closeness a hard body could.

"I don't know, but it was damn good."

"That's why I can't believe you don't engage in frequent sex."

"One thing I do know is me, and I can be good to me baby. I don't have to worry about me deceiving me," I said. His mouth fell open. "Openness and honesty are so important to me and finding a man who is willing to be true to the game is practically unheard of. If we plan to do this again I have to have your word that you will be just that."

"Yeah, those things are important to me too."

"The biggest mistake I will probably ever make with you is what I just did, have sex unprotected. I don't know you and even if I did, that doesn't make you immune to something deadly. It's unrealistic to think of us as nothing more than a couple of people who share an attraction. I don't have any expectations, other than openness, honesty and respect. We are separated by hundreds of miles and I don't expect for you to reserve yourself for me, but I do expect you to use selection, discretion, and protection when giving other opportunity a place on your welcome mat."

Ricky's amazed look was apparent. Before he could speak I placed my index finger over his dry, exhausted lips.

"The only thing I ask is if you find another woman who matches what I have to give, and is rolling past me, that you let me know out of respect," I said. "And if I find my knight soaring toward me I'll do the same, especially if I let him draw his sword. You'll be the first to know because that would end us. I don't do two men at the same time but I understand because a lot of people can."

He lifted my finger from his lips. "You can't be serious. This type of shit only happens in the movies Michelle. You are telling me to get my groove on?"

"I'm telling you that I don't expect a sense of obligation based simply on intimacy. When two people meet and share romance that doesn't mean they were meant to be. Keep it real, you know what I mean?"

"So that means you go to Nashville and live it up right?"

"No, actually it means that all doors remain open, with no road blocks. Why should a person feel like they can not or should not pursue a connection because they are casually spoken for, they might be turning down a match made in heaven. If I indulge in a relationship it has to be written by God. If I am given a new page to turn I will turn it, know what I mean?"

"This has to be a first. A female who wants or expects a man to do his do. You are not just radiant, you're different, and your personality is an award winner. You can mingle and kick it, crack jokes, and you like to laugh. You screw like a champ and when your feet touch the floor I know you will be as graceful as you were earlier. What more would any man ask for?" he said with a bit of an attitude.

"I refuse to be untrue to the game. My daddy taught me to keep it real, always. Deal?"

"Deal."

I offered my index finger to him. "Don't take this the wrong way, but you have no idea who you just got involved with. Let's seal the vow with a finger shake," I said.

He connected his finger to mine and we waved them back and forth. I leaned over to Ricky and kissed him tenderly. I could sense the hesitation and confusion he felt, but it was all good.

# Chapter 11

When my eyes opened, I had to adjust my mind and remember where I was. Ricky was already up, so I made the bed. I took my overnight bag in the bathroom, showered and changed into my sweats to wear on the road.

When I walked in the living room, Ricky was at the dining room table drinking a glass of orange juice. There was no music playing and the television wasn't on. I heated a cup of water in the microwave and made myself a strong cup of instant coffee, and ate my Payday. I sat in the chair across from him and quickly realized why he was sitting in silence. He was listening to Danita in the other bedroom reading something to Darryl that I had written.

"..Never be afraid to delete a useless file or program, which will likely be disguised as a person, place, or thing. Keep your trash emptied. Never forget that no data is ever gone completely, so refrain from doing anything you would not be proud for Him to see. Keep in mind, a journey was planned, and this is merely an experience our soul is having.

"Believe strongly in God. Trust your driving force, and follow His lead. Let's work to find our purpose, proceed in spirit, and allow our actions to be guided by the mysterious force of the Holy Spirit through instinct. Our mission to defy death by way of our planned journey is possible.

"With that having been said, I would like to welcome you aboard flight 007, with first class service through your planned journey, providing non-stop service to everlasting life. Fasten your seat belt, our departure is set to begin. We have entered the runway to life. We are fueled with the love of God, and our travel is through the beauty of the mind, body, and soul. Our final destination, eternity. We are now ready for take off," Danita read.

The look on Ricky's face was curious. Danita and Darryl walked into the living room where they quickly realized the opener to the tool box had been heard by everyone.

Darryl had a GQ look. He wore a Fila sweat suit, and the same brand gym shoes. His dark chocolate skin was smooth and his round face was clean shaven. His hair was dark and wavy, and cut short. His small round eyeglasses made him look intellectual.

"You are a damn deep writer," Darryl said.

"Hi my name is Michelle. So did you like it?" I asked.

"Yes I did, a lot. I'm Darryl," he said. "You should be a motivational speaker. Did you hear that Rick?"

"Yeah," Ricky said.

"Thought provoking best describes it," I said. "It is the best medicine for the mind, leaving the reader in control. My only goal is to plant the seed."

"Danita said you wrote that for teenagers, but I know some adults who could benefit from that, me being one of them," Darryl said.

"It's a box of tools she's designing to assist in finding your personal legacy," Danita said.

"Somehow I knew it was yours when I heard some of the first words," Ricky said.

"I'm glad you enjoyed it, but that is only the opener, I have so much more to say. My insides are running over with expressions I want to share," I said.

"Share," Darryl said.

"We are faced with walking a battlefield during this human experience, because the good is mixed with evil. You can be on the winning team by being armed with your belief system, and by avoiding lurking danger. Life is filled with so many lessons, that we must accept our role as student. Once a lesson is learned you have to move forward. Moving on with our lives is probably the greatest challenge, but success is living God's purpose. We must develop an obligation to His plan and commit to it, by making that special connection and allowing your actions to be guided.

"You can make the commitment by offering Him an unbeatable lease agreement, by making your heart, a sound peaceful place where he can work without interruption. You have a personal guide in instinct, the best friend that was given to all of us. That is your link to the Holy Spirit. The decor He selects is designed especially for you, and there is no other person with a place like yours. You are unique and the relationship you develop with God is by special design."

"Okay, that was your Sunday morning service on Saturday afternoon. Collection plate please," Danita said laughing. She picked up the plate on the dining room table and tried to hand it to Darryl.

"You are going to have these brothas afraid of me," I said. I took the plate from her and put it back on the table. "That is not unheard of you know."

"I was trying share some of your magic with Darryl, I didn't know Ricky was up."

"Keep going," Darryl said.

"If you have accepted the invitation, God's' presence is in your heart. He has set up shop to decorate the walls. If He used blood, He would stroke the surface with His hand. If you don't follow His lead, He will go over the same spot until you allow your actions to be guided by that power. The movement of His hand is guided by the action mechanism, the over sighted sense. We live, we learn through lesson, and we must move on. Instinct is your connection to the channel. If He is attempting to take you to the road that leads to your destiny and you are not following the lead you were given, He can't begin to cover the surface. He needs your help in order to get your place ready for you. Unless you want to come back and do this all over again, you'll do it right this time by letting Him finish the job," I said. "Okay, that's enough."

"Don't stop now," Darryl said.

I looked at Ricky, he looked amazed, but I knew he was absorbing my words like a sponge.

"This process has to be done in stages, not all at once. There are seven tools. First you have to add a sense of God, the action mechanism to your other five senses. Next you have to acknowledge and trust instinct. Third, you have to be willing to follow your lead and take risks. Just trust that you have an insurance policy. Your agent is your guardian angel. Once you know the spiritual side of yourself you have to separate the soul from the shell and live in spirit. Your shell is only your vehicle for human life. Live only in spirit through the harmony of the connection you gain. When this magical event takes place you will feel reborn. It is then that you will notice your close encounters of a different kind. You will meet people who you were destined to meet for a reason. It is through those encounters where you will be able to unlock and utilize your hidden magic. That magic can best be described as walking in your life's purpose, the way I feel about writing. Then you have to work to keep your tools in working order to keep yourself on the path. After that, it's destination destiny."

"Well, was this or was it not a service?" Danita asked.

"You sure you can handle a mind like this Ricky? I don't see how you can't be mystified by her," Darryl said.

"Man, you have no idea," Ricky said shaking his head. "You have no idea."

# Chapter 12

We were over halfway back to Nashville when I decided I was tired of driving. The sight of cars in front of me, were turning into a blurry image. I felt a sleepiness taking over. We stopped right outside Atlanta and filled the tank. I got another small cup of coffee, and a candy bar. I climbed in the passenger seat and adjusted the seat for relaxation.

"Girl, why was Eric as fine as vintage wine?" I asked.

"I know that's right," Danita said. "He's not my type though, but Darryl, now that is something to consider."

We met Ricky's roommate on our way out. Eric was so fine. He was tall and built. I don't usually look twice at light brothas, but damn, this brotha looked like a great work of Asian art dipped in chocolate. Where was he that night at the club? He was upbeat and energetic, and had a great sense of humor.

I dug around in my duffel bag and pulled out my dream journal to record my dream from the previous night.

♠

*It All Makes Sense*

*A strange man is telling me to come with him. He tells me he is supposed to tell me to turn to page 12 and he started to sing Mary Had A Little Lamb. I realize my dream is a lucid one. A lady there tells me he is crazy. I tell her I am a dreamer, and it makes sense to me. I see Spencer, who comes in the room with a bag filled with baby toys. Later, I am the fourth car in a four car accident. I notice some brown stuff across my stomach. I am wearing a pouch. I awake.*

I turned to the twelfth page of the new journal I had started the day I arrived in Florida. The dream on page twelve was, It's Like Magic. "Danita, you are not going to believe this, listen," I said. I read my newest dream to her and went back to page 12. "I titled this one, It's Like Magic."

◆

*A man standing outside in the very bright sun is telling me to come this way. I realize I am having a lucid dream. I am driving in a car with three other women. We see a sign that says Winter Park with an arrow pointing to the left. We are going to a casino to gamble, and to celebrate a birthday. I have a hard time picking out an outfit to wear, because I think most of the clothes I have with me are for work. I finally find a jumpsuit that is emerald green and has gold angels all over it. I am sitting in the driver's seat of the car looking in the rearview mirror where I do my hair and makeup.*

"Danita, I wore a green dress the other night at the nightclub in Winter Park, and I did my hair and make up in the car."

"Not to mention that gold fingernail polish you're wearing," she said. "Michelle, that's deep."

I read to myself until I came to the "The Mystery Man" dream.

"Danita, check this out. You are not going to believe this," I said. I placed my hand over my heart in sheer amazement and read the dream to her.

"Oh my God Michelle, that just happened at the arena!

The man you couldn't see was Ricky," she said.

"What do you think this means?"

"It has to mean it was fate that brought you together."

"I can't tell him this. He'll think I'm crazy. I think he was uncomfortable this morning when he heard my story and after my sermon."

"So? You said yourself, everything happens for a reason I think I would tell him."

"No, I think not. I don't want to scare him off."

"I think it's because you know you're too deep for him," she said.

"Maybe you're right. I don't know what this encounter will bring to the table, but whatever role I have in it, I want to be ready."

"I've never known of you not to be."

I was speechless. Danita was talking, but I was so dumbfounded I didn't hear a word she said. How could I dream of Ricky before meeting him? Who was he? Why was the dream a lucid one? Questions flooded my mind, and the answers seemed a drought. I could not believe it. I was in such a state of shock all I could do was to stop reading and lay my head back on the headrest. I dozed off to sleep and didn't awake until we were fifty miles from home.

We walked in the house to a flashing caller ID that signaled voice mail messages were waiting. Danita sorted through the tall stack of mail, and headed straight for the kitchen and made some hot tea. I picked up the phone to call Ricky.

"Hey baby," he said. "How was your trip home?"

"It was quite relaxing. I had a chance to really unwind

from the weekend. You sound excited. What's up?"

"Get a pen and take down this number," he said. "I got a toll free pager for you to keep in touch. You can send me text, numeric, or voice. The offer is still good if you decide you'd rather be in Florida."

I got a pen and took down the number.

"Well I just wanted to let you know we made it here safely. I can't wait to see you again," I said.

"I miss you already. We play next Friday night. Do you think you can come down for that?"

"I don't think so," I said. "I do have to get myself settled in the Nashville mode. I have to update my resume and get out in the daily stretch to pay the bills."

"Okay," he said. "I'll miss you, and I want to see you as soon as possible."

When I hung up the phone I tested the pager and left a text message, "Don't forget our vow. Keep it real"

I wasn't sure why this was happening to me, but I had to practice the same thing I try hard to preach. It was none of my business, because this is His business. I stretched out across my bed and studied a few entries in my journal.

◆

*It's Show Time*

*I am looking for my friend Michael, before I find him I try to clear everyone out of the room. I look up and see him standing in the doorway asking why I wanted to see him. I tell him I wanted to say good-bye before I moved to Minneapolis. He tells me I won't be able to make it while I'm only making a small amount of money. Michael looks over my bills and says, "Damn how much is Show Time?"*

♥

*Scavenger Hunt*

*Michael has a new game. I think it is scavenger hunt. All of these brothas are excited about playing this child's game. We are climbing to the top of a building and are left to find our way back. There are lots of players. I know Lisa is there.*

♣

*Just Give It To Me*

*I am telling Darrin that I have to go for it, that I don't care if it is a 56 or 57. I had to repeat it twice before he understands what I'm saying. Finally, me and Lisa leave and find some green nail polish on or around mama's grave.*

Without warning, my eyes grew heavy, like they were telling me that was enough. I closed my journal and put it on the night stand. The only thing I could connect was the number fifty seven. I looked in the Arenaball Magazine I had gotten from Ricky and confirmed it was his jersey number.

I didn't want to wrap myself into trying to make my dreams something they may not be. I looked up the meanings to some of the symbols in my dream dictionary to find their significance. I have believed for a number of years, there is buried treasure to be found in dreams. Understanding their purpose gave me a sense of fulfillment and guidance. I had begun giving my dreams titles to sum up the initial feeling I got from them the instant they occurred.

I let out a deep yawn. I lit my inner spirit, vitality candle and switched off my lamp. I laid across my daybed, folded my pillow, and stuffed it under my head. I thought again about what I was embarking upon, and tried to focus on being prepared, instead of the specifics of what the role was. I replayed each of my seven tools in my head and thought about how well they were polished. I had to make sure I was using them for the purpose intended. I prayed before a deep meditation session and fell asleep.

# Chapter 13

I got settled with the life I was making for myself in Nashville rather smoothly. I updated my resume and put my professional wheels into motion to secure employment. I searched in the financial market as well as administration and landed a position the second day in Commercial Client Services at BellSouth in the heart of downtown.

I had my own small office and was assigned a group of clients who's needs were easily identified and who weren't too demanding. My space on the fifteenth floor overlooked the stadium for the Titans on the Cumberland river front. The ugly sight of a bridge near the stadium was under rapid construction, or some serious modification.

I rearranged my modern three drawer desk to face the door and carefully arranged my two file cabinets in front of the window behind me where I put two blooming plants and some family photos. The glass partisans that divided the offices defeated the purpose of privacy.

Most everyone in our offices used their file cabinets as a privacy shield to block the view from their neighbors, placing one on each side. I had intentionally moved my file cabinets so that I could see my neighbors. I sat between Brandy, a Prince and martial arts fanatic, and Corena, a country girl who loved to laugh. Brandy was a tall thin light sister with light brown hair that she wore in a late eighties mushroom style. Corena was the color of a Hershey bar with a slight case of acne that looked like hidden almonds. Corena was into her man Clem like a young school girl in love for the first time. They were both fun and we always laughed at how the three Afreecas, that we named ourselves, were seated together in the line of fire among the rest of our white coworkers.

It was a Friday, and nearly time to wrap up the week. I picked up the phone and called Ricky.

"Hello," Ricky said.

"Hey Ricky. What are you up to?"

"Nothing."

"Why are you sounding so dry?"

"Michelle, I keep thinking about the things you said to me about what you want with us. It seems that you don't want anything."

"I want to enjoy getting to know you," I said with a sweet tone.

"I think we should know what we are going to do before either one of us brings someone else in the picture."

"Ricky, what I want is what I asked you for. I don't expect you to suppress your urges though. If we find that we are meant to be, time will tell. There is no need to force a drive. Let's just enjoy the ride. What we've done here is a lot like opening a joint bank account. As long as you put into it more than you try and gain, the interest will continue to grow," I said. "Or, if you'd rather we can close it up and call it a day."

"No, I want to keep it open," he said. "I can agree to take it one day at a time."

"Well, I'm still at work so I'll call you later."

"No, let me call you. Page me when you get some time later."

"Okay, bye."

"Later."

I hung up the phone and finished up some work for the following week to make myself a mild Monday. I watered my plants and dusted the furniture. The night skies were making their debut for the evening when I finally clocked out for the week and submitted my time card.

Me and my girls headed to the elevator where we ran into some more coworkers. They invited me and Brandy to join them for cocktails at Mere Bulles to unwind from the demanding attention of the work week. Corena headed home where she always seemed to spend the weekends, on lock down with her man.

After a few drinks, Brandy and I left the lounge together and walked to the parking garage. The downtown streets of Nashville had started to fill with tourists and country music lovers. I headed to Ed's, a locally owned fish joint north of downtown for a fish sandwich and fries before heading home. Ed's was packed. Cars were lined in the drive through, and was backed up on D B Todd Boulevard. I had a weekend of writing planned and took some notes of my thoughts on my little hand held recorder while I waited in the long line.

A normal weekend routine spent in Nashville usually included a Friday night of kicking it, and a Saturday night appearance at Yesterday's. Danita and I made our frequent appearances in the night life while our circle of friends grew to include some real cool people who we would sometimes get together with on Sundays to watch sports over drinks.

I sat in front of my computer until Danita broke my self induced trance late Saturday afternoon with a plan to go out to the club.

Yesterday's was packed as always. We started the evening with a few rounds of pool while we downed a few starter drinks. The music sounded better and louder the more drinks we put down.

We had just sat down at a table near the dance floor when Terry came over to introduce his friend Justin to us. Terry was a slight shorty who didn't quite meet with a six foot frame and probably barely tipped the scales over one sixty. He was actually kind of fine. His skin was the color of creamed coffee, he wore a goat tee and a low haircut. His rather tone physique made his clothes fit him to a tee. He wore a pair of nicely pressed jeans with a plain white silk shirt that was only buttoned halfway and some cowboy boots with sharp pointed toes.

"You feel like dancing Michelle?" Terry asked.

"Yeah," I said. "Let's go."

Me and Terry danced for several songs. Danita and Justin selected a booty song to groove to just when Terry and I headed for the table for another drink.

"Do you date?" Terry asked. "I know I asked you this before, all you said was that you keep busy."

"I guess you can say I am available to date."

"Let me take you to dinner one night next week."

"Okay, I'd like that."

I quickly realized that Ricky's image was not in my head the way I thought it would be especially since I had dreamed him up. The thoughts of him in my head grew less frequent and more distorted as I fell in a great comfort zone in my new home town. There was no way I could grow easily bored with all the young, attractive, available brothas that kept my eyes on high alert.

# Chapter 14

I ignored the sound of the telephone ringing to try and hang on to the good sleep I had the night before. My legs were sore from my new work out routine. I gave them a hard stretch when I rolled over.

"Michelle," Danita yelled up the stairs. "Telephone."

I reached over to pick up the receiver when my stomach suddenly became sensitive to the smell of bacon that had drifted up the stairs to my bedroom. It was Saturday morning, the one day when Danita always made a hot breakfast. I looked up at the African art I had hung on my bare walls just days before.

"Hello?"

"Hey baby doll," Ricky said. "Did I wake you?"

"Yes, but that's okay," I said. "What's up?"

"I can't get you off my mind. I wanted to hear your voice."

"Oh, that's sweet."

"I thought I might persuade you to come and see me this weekend."

"You know how expensive it is to fly without notice," I said. "Anyway, it's Saturday. How about next weekend. I don't feel good anyway."

"Okay, that's a bet. Do you want me to make the arrangements?"

"No, I'll take care of it. I need to take care of some

business there anyway."

"What business do you have here besides me?"

"Wouldn't you like to know," I joked. "I need to see my friend Scott."

"Who is this dude?" Ricky asked. "Is this someone who is interested in you?"

"No silly, I told you he's a writer and we're friends."

"Well if I pay for this trip, I want you to myself."

"Well I guess you just saved yourself a fat face Franklin because I need to make the trip beneficial if I can."

"Michelle, I don't understand you," he said. "What's really going on?"

"Ricky, I told you in the beginning that I need my space, that.." I paused when I felt the nausea about to explode. "Ricky, I'm getting sick. I'll call you back."

I held my hand over my mouth and rushed in the bathroom. The watery vomit spilled out of my mouth like a running faucet. What a way to start my weekend, with a damn flu bug. I washed my face, brushed the funk off my teeth and went downstairs. I felt hot, and now that Freeze had moved out I could lounge around in comfort without my robe. When I walked in the living room, I straightened the picture of Jesus that always seemed to find a way to lay on the wall in a slanted position.

"Hey Michelle, I'm just about to hook up some waffles, "Danita said. "Want some?"

"No. I just got sick upstairs, I think it was the smell of the bacon."

"Maybe it was that hot Princess chicken you had last night. I don't see how you eat that stuff."

"Yeah, maybe. I know I'm not hungover, I only had three beers."

I got myself a bottled water out of the refrigerator, turned on cartoon network and laid on the couch. Danita came in with her plate piled high and sat on the love seat. As soon as the water hit my stomach I was sick again. I ran to the downstairs bathroom and closed the door. I wet a washcloth, and wiped my face. Danita was coming down the stairs with my pillow and a blanket for me.

"Michelle, you never get sick," Danita said. "Do you think you might be pregnant?"

I raised up off the couch, and rested my head in the palms of my hands. "When is our period due?" I asked. Danita and I had our cycles at the same time and I never kept up with it.

"I'm on my second day now," she said. "I bet Ricky is not really fixed. That just doesn't make sense. He's young, not married, I know he has a child but why would he make a decision like that at his age?"

"I usually start my period before you. I bet you're right. That no good sonofabitch," I said.

"I'll run up to Walgreen's after I get dressed and get you an EPT," she said. "I bet you are pregnant Michelle. Remember the dream you had, when the man was singing Mary had a little lamb?"

"Oh my God, that's right. It All Makes Sense," I said. "My guess is this test is only a formality."

It was near noon when Danita returned home from the store. When she opened the door I felt the brisk breeze from the frigid wind on the cool fall afternoon. I went to my bedroom, and sat in the middle of my day bed. I used the crumpled covers as a table while I read the directions on how to use the test.

After I finished the test, I placed the stick on the back of the toilet and went to make my bed. I knew more than five minutes had passed. I put my hand over my forehead and let out a sigh of fear. My palms felt sweaty. I looked out the door and into the bathroom where the clouded sun casted a faint light that barely lit the room. The fuchsia colored plus sign glared me in the face when I leaned over to look at the test window. I heard Danita coming up the stairs.

"Well?" she asked.

I picked up the stick and handed it to her.

"I knew it," she said.

"It's bad enough that I stooped to sex as quickly as I did," I said. "What a price to pay, to go as long as I had without sex and to end up pregnant."

Hurt and disappointed feelings consumed me the entire day. There was no way I was going to tell Ricky over the phone. I called Southwest airlines and made a reservation to fly to Florida the coming Thursday. When I called Ricky to tell him when I would be arriving it felt like having a conversation with a total stranger.

# Chapter 15

I took in a deep breath of the Florida air after my flight touched down in Orlando. I let the top down on the red rag top rental, and came out of the sweatshirt, and sweats I had worn to keep me warm on the chilly November day in Nashville. I made a quick conversion into a sky blue, fitted, short outfit I had worn underneath. I changed from my tennis shoes to my toe revealing sandals.

Ricky was aware of the time of my plane's arrival, and was expecting me any minute. I made a pit stop at TJMaxx to look in the jewelry case for the ring I had seen back home.

Staring me in the face was the ring I wanted, a silver toe ring that symbolized my passion, the sun, moon, and stars. My appetite was defined by the unknown, and this ring was a true reflection of my personality. Luckily they had it in my size.

Ricky had prepared a romantic dinner. A long stem candle was sitting in the middle of the round glass table. Its flame was flickering, casting shadows on the wall. A bowl of strawberries were soaked in a pool of whipped cream sitting next to a chilled bottle of Sutter Home that was wrapped in a white linen napkin.

Ricky wore only a pair of blue silk boxers. His chocolate body glowed in the dimly lit apartment that was always neat and clean like he staffed a merry maid. His legs, a blueprint of legs from paradise with protruding thighs, and molded calves, were the look of flawless art. His bare chest revealed his rock hard six pack. He greeted me with a kiss and tight hug, but wanted to know what took me so long.

"I stopped to pick up this ring in my size," I said. I lifted up my bare leg, and placed it in his hand. I wiggled my gold painted toes.

"Why can't you come here just for me?" Ricky asked. "You always have something to do."

I ignored the comment, and went to change the CD player from a begging Keith Sweat to a smooth Sade since Ricky didn't stock any jazz. I wanted to make the mood just right, and her calm lyrics were a soothing flavor that instantly transmitted relaxation to the atmosphere.

"How was your flight?" he asked.

"Relaxing," I said. "I get so lost in my thoughts, and there is no better place to meditate."

"You mediate often don't you?"

"Every peaceful moment a day can bring. You wouldn't believe the difference it makes when you learn the art of living in the spirit."

Ricky poured the wine, and handed me my glass.

"I want to make a toast," he said. "I am so glad that you came into my life for whatever reason. Here's to you"

We gently touched our glasses that echoed like a soft chime.

"Do you think you know the reason?"

"Well, I thought about it, and I just think that you are an incredible person."

"No, not person, I'd rather be referred to as a being."

"Do you always have to complicate words?"

"Words are what makes me, me. It's not complicated, and neither am I. If you paid attention you would find relevance."

"Every friend of mine who has met you have said the same thing as me, that there's just something about you, something different."

"I take that as a compliment," I said. "Thank you."

"You're welcome."

I poured the rest of the wine in my mouth. Ricky refilled my glass, and stared me in the face.

"Ricky do you believe in fate?" I asked.

"Fate?" He asked. He paused for a moment, and decided to refill his own glass. "I guess if I had evidence that dreams can come true, I would."

"Anything is possible, as long as your heart is in it, but so many people get blinded by the things they want instead of focusing on what it is they need."

"What is it that you need?"

"The love of God."

"And?"

"That's it, the rest is inevitable. I allow the driving forces to steer my direction. I like to think that I'm in the driver's seat, but I know I'm just here for the ride. Sometimes things get a little foggy, but that's when I need meditation, when I lose focus. My eye is always in search of the prize."

After a rib-eye steak dinner made just right in Ricky's George Foreman grill, baked sweet potatoes, and slow roasted Italian green beans, I went to change the CD to Aaliyah. I made the open space on the living room floor a stage where I started a strip tease to One In A Million.

I watched Ricky's every move while he loaded the dishwasher. I untied my half top and moved my lips to the words of the song. My hair tickled my arm pits when I took the shirt off my shoulders. My powder blue bra gave my medium sized breasts a boost of wonder.

Ricky put down the dishes, walked in the room and leaned his back against the breakfast nook. I threw my shirt like a scarf over his head and ran my hands down his chest and kissed each one of his hard nipples. When I heard the sound of Eric's key in the door, I pulled my shirt from around Ricky's neck and blew him a kiss and dashed to his bedroom.

I took a quick shower and put on my green g-string teddy with tiny star sequin that had screamed Ricky's name when I was packing my overnight bag.

I thought again about what I came to tell him. I had tried to open my mouth earlier, but choked on the words during dinner. When I walked out of the bathroom, Ricky was lying in his bed with his arms locked together behind his head, a pose that proved to be his trademark.

"Damn baby, that is a loud green," he said.

"It is kind of loud huh? No wonder it was screaming your name from my dresser drawer."

I reached for his arms and sat him up on the side of the bed. Just minutes into my lap dance, I remembered again my reason for coming. Ricky's manhood had already responded to my boldness, something he had liked about me at first, but it was clearly become intimidating to him.

"Ricky, I mean Mr. Vasectomy," I said. "I'm pregnant."

"What?" he asked. He looked at me like I was speaking a foreign language.

"Why did you lie to me?" I asked. "Did you think that I was involved with men other than just you, and if I became pregnant you could deny it? I told you I can't have an intimate relationship with more than one man. It's not like I was trying to make you my man, it's just not my style."

"Damn," he said. Ricky rubbed his bald head with the palms of both hands. "Are you okay with it? The pregnancy I mean."

"I'm pissed off because you lied about the vasectomy."

"I told you how I felt about you, I was truthful about that," he said.

After a brief pause he looked up at me. His curly eye lashes touched his eyelids. His brown eyes looked sad. "So now would you think about coming here to stay?" he asked.

Before I knew it, my hand smacked Ricky across his face. "What is this? This is some stunt a female would pull, not a niggah."

After several minutes of a tennis match argument filled with words of anger, and frustration, we embraced each other with tenderness. As mad as I was, I needed his comfort.

"Can we get back to the lap dance," Ricky whispered in her ear. "Put that loud green thing into motion."

"This money green thing has secret that came from Victoria. I think she's trying to tell you to keep your eye on the ball." I put his chin in the palm of my hand. As my eager grind met with his bare chest, he buried his face in between my breasts, and kissed my cleavage.

I watched his eyes roam over my body. I could see the flicker from the glittery sequin from my teddy sparkle in his eyes. I turned my back to him, and put his hands on top of my thighs while I backed up to his thrusting dick.

All I could do was repeat those words in a low whisper, "Keep your eye on the ball baby, just keep your eye on the ball."

I knew Ricky hated when I used words that wore on his mind but I loved planting seeds. I could feel his hands slightly shaking. Tiny beads of sweat had collected on his forehead.

I knew his thoughts were flooded, and would run on replay over, and over again, even after I left. Whatever my reasons for saying the things I did, I tried to never mind the matter and leave it to my mind and soul handle the situation. He moaned with excitement and enjoyed my sensuous body.

I was so lost in the moment, I forgot that I was carrying his child. I rode him like a rodeo queen. The blinks of the glitter flashed in his eyes, casting before me, the star studded night.

# Chapter 16

My situation was becoming more complicated by the minute. Every thoughtless moment my mind could find, inflated the big ball of confusion growing in my head. My mind was trapped in constant thought. I never imagined that I would be faced with such a big decision. I tried to sleep through my entire flight home.

When I walked in the house I looked up at the portrait above the fireplace. I felt like a little kid who got caught with their hand in the cookie jar. My humbled eyes turned away from Jesus.

I took a nap until late Sunday evening. It was nearly nine when I came downstairs. Danita was putting the slow cooker on the counter. I poured myself a tall glass of milk, and heated up some microwave pancakes that I smothered in syrup.

"I am no closer to knowing what I'm going to do than I was before I left," I said.

"You know that God will not give you more than you can bear," Danita replied.

"I'm praying about it. I just can't see going through this right after my move to a new city. I don't even have my own place yet. I'm just not ready to be a mother." I listened to my own words as salty tasting tear drops wet my lips. "I can't see Ricky being there for me with his flaky ass. I see now why I can go without. Drama is attached to any dick."

"Whatever you decide to do," Danita said, "I'm here for you."

I knew Danita didn't want to persuade me either way. She stood at the stove with her hand planted on her hip, stirring the sizzling ground beef. She turned and started piling her fixings together in the slow cooker to cook overnight. Finally I broke the silence.

"Okay. I'm going to schedule an abortion first thing tomorrow morning just in case I decide to terminate. If I do, I want to get it over with as quickly as possible. I'll call Ricky and tell him that I think I'm going to have an abortion. His lying ass should pay for the whole thing, but I'll settle for half."

Over the next several weeks, I shed a lot of tears. Ricky had agreed to pay for half the cost of an abortion, although his whole tone toward me changed like the weather.

The day I dreaded felt a day I did not even live. I felt like I was sleep walking through the entire day. I didn't even feel attached to my own skin. I figured the traumatic episode was the reason I felt so lost inside. I felt an instant impact on my life after the procedure. For weeks following the procedure, I did not have a single dream.

Feeling consumed with hurt, confused, regretful feelings, I made time for a moment of serenity to share with God. I drew myself a bath, and surrounded the bathtub with candles. I prayed as hard, and as deep and I knew how. I cried as I never had before. I begged that if I had done something against the will of God that He would forgive me. After going to bed I meditated my way to a peaceful sleep. That night my drought with dreaming broke.

♥

*Touched by an Angel*

*I am standing in a pool of clouds and what looks like smoke. My deceased Uncle Kenneth is standing there with me. He looks the way he did when he was in his best of health. We were speaking to each other, but neither of our mouths were moving. I told him how much I felt like an isolated incident. I told him I sometimes felt like a case of Touched By An Angel. I told him I did try to stay connected but I felt so different. He held my hands in his and said that I was doing just fine. He assured me that I was on track and I was where I was supposed to be right now He convinced me that I was doing just fine, and when he thought I was okay with it he disappeared. I awake.*

I sat up in my bed, and replayed the dream in my head. I prayed a prayer of thanks for the encounter with my uncle that I was sure was somehow real. I turned on my bedroom light, and opened my briefcase. I took out some tapes I had recorded of my thoughts. I looked at the titles, and put one in my recorder that was marked, The Very Thought, and pushed play. It was a tape I made before I ever left Illinois. I listened to my own voice on the tape, still groggy from just waking up telling a dream I had the night before.

♠

*"I am in a house where Bobby and Regina are preparing dinner. I am sitting on the couch watching a game on TV. The house is unfamiliar, and has lots of windows that overlook a big field. I*

*notice a powder blue bible on the table. All of a sudden I wonder what's for dinner, and when I turn to ask, Bobby and Regina have turned into Danita and Freeze."*

My mouth fell wide open, Bobby and Regina changed into Danita and Freeze. I left Florida, and came to stay with Danita and Freeze in Nashville. I turned off my recorder. For me, the words on the recorder validated my dream.

I quickly thought about Scott, who I still hadn't told I left Florida. I thought now would be a good time to tell him. I could get rid of my voice mail that for months had only been used for the purpose of communicating with him. It was only twenty after one on a Friday night, so I picked up the cordless phone and dialed Scott's number. I was preparing to leave a voice mail when I heard Scott's deep voice.

"Holla at me," Scott said.

"Hey Scott what's going on?" I asked.

"Hey Michelle, I was just thinking about you, and how odd it was that I hadn't seen you. Nobody had seen you at the gym lately either. Is everything okay?"

"Yes, everything is fine." I had normally dialed star 67 before calling Scott so the call would come up as unknown. This time I dialed straight through, and picked up that Scott wasn't looking at the caller ID. "I'm in Nashville."

"Why Nashville?" Scott asked. "Ain't that the country music capital of the planet?"

"It might be to some, but R & B stands for refined and black. It's actually pretty cool."

"I figured something had happened to you when you didn't

get back with me. Did you get my voice mails?"

"I haven't checked them lately. I've been caught up with some other drama lately," I said.

"I read the material you left my way. I gotta say girl, you have a deep ass way of thinking. Sometimes you go deeper than I'm prepared for, but I came out okay. I can't wait for you to see some of my comments."

"Can you mail it to me? Give me your address because I got some more stuff for you to see. Don't you have anything for me?"

"Michelle I have been so deep into your stuff that I'm droughting with writer's block."

"Is my work distracting you?" I asked. "I mean, we can chill."

"No way baby girl, I am having the time of my life exploring that mysterious mind of yours. I think you will find some of my comments useful."

We exchanged addresses. I reminded Scott to get the number off the caller ID. I had been hesitant, and wasn't sure how Scott would react to my move, especially after all the conversations we had about faith, and living in the spirit. I thought I had gone against the elements I always preached about to the one person besides Danita who seemed to make a difference when it came to understanding me. I had a trust and admiration for Scott and his writing knowledge. The time had come to let him know where I was, since I knew for sure I was right on track.

# Chapter 17

Danita and I boarded a flight to Orlando the weekend of my birthday. I wanted to party and Danita wanted to see Darryl so we planned to spend Friday night with him in Palm Bay.

I gazed out the window in deep thought. Ricky was rude the last time I talked to him. It sounded like he had a party going on with some little kids' voices in the background. I knew he was not sure what to make of me and I know I can be hard to take, but why was he suddenly rude? If he wanted to end our relationship. I would make sure he would grow the balls and do it like a man.

I sat in my seat with my eyes closed and realized that I could count the times I had seen Ricky. I couldn't believe how I could dream him up and the situation end up like it did. Every time I rolled into the city of Orlando was like walking on the set of an ongoing movie.

Danita and I had gone out with Ricky's roommate Eric the last time we had come. We were there to get clothes for the cold weather that had set in Nashville. Ricky was headed out for a camp when we arrived and I only saw him for a few minutes, but he welcomed us to stay at his house while he was gone. When we went out that night I felt like I was being watched. I ended up leaving Eric and Danita at the club, and going to see Scott.

I read my journal on the way back home after that visit and came across a dream where Danita and I were at the club in the same clothes we really wore that night. The only difference was that in the dream, Ricky was at the club, and he pushed my hands away when I tried to hug him.

My dreams continued to come to pass, at least one with every visit. Every time it was happening in my waking life I had no memory of the dreams.

I continued to play out the role I was handed and gave little thought to the reasons for my unexplained actions and behavior.

The change of weather was like night and day. January in Nashville held on to frosty nights and chilly days. Orlando was muggy and hot like it was the middle of summer.

We stopped at the mall when we arrived in Palm Bay to pick up the keys to Darryl's apartment. Darryl walked out of the shoe store he managed when he saw us. I knew I wasn't one of his favorite people. He thought I was too much of an influence over Danita since they had started a fling.

"Hey Red," Darryl said. He embraced Danita. "Hi Michelle."

"What's up Darryl?" I sensed that Darryl didn't care for me. That was quite a change since he was so impressed with me when we met. I was sure he thought I was playing games with Ricky's mind.

"Have you talked to Rick?" Darryl asked.

"No, I haven't." I knew Darryl had already informed Ricky that I was coming even though I told Danita to tell him not to.

"I thought it might be cool if Rick came down here. We could get some dinner and chill at my place."

"I don't know about yall, but I'm going out. I'm not in the

mood to chill. Did you tell Ricky I was coming?"

"No. Danita asked me not to," Darryl said.

"Good, then I don't have to explain my whereabouts," I said. I knew some drama was brewing when Darryl said Ricky didn't know I was there. They were best friends, and there was no way I believed that.

Danita and I were getting dressed for a night out on the town when Darryl walked in the door after work.

"Yall are really going out?" Darryl asked.

"Yes. This is her birthday weekend and I'm going to kick it with her, with or without you," Danita said.

"Where are yall going?"

"Orlando," Danita said.

"Well I wanted to spend time with you, so I'll come too," Darryl said.

"That's cool," Danita said.

Everything was going according to plan until we piled in Darryl's car and he drove aimlessly for an hour or so.

"Is Orlando this far?" I asked.

"I was trying to take a short cut," Darryl said. "I have no idea where I am."

For the next hour we drove around in what seemed to be circles, until I spotted the toll road.

"Um, there's the toll Darryl," I said.

"I don't want to pay for the toll road," Darryl said.

"Well I'll pay for it," I said. "I'm sick of riding."

Darryl kept on going nowhere and apparently he forgot that I was familiar with Orlando. I knew the night was going nowhere just like Darryl, and played lost too. When I spotted

436, the highway Ricky lived on, I pointed it out.

"There's 436 Darryl. Doesn't Ricky live on this road?" I tried to think my directions through and pointed the way I thought was wrong. "I think it's that way."

Okay, this niggah thinks I'm stupid. He's trying to keep us away from Orlando. Well, niggah a player can't be played. It's your gas, go for it, I thought.

By the time we arrived back at Darryl's house I had fallen asleep and was awakened to hear Darryl and Danita fussing over the time we had wasted, dressed, and ready party.

"Oh, that was fun." I climbed out of the back seat of Darryl's car and into my rental.

"Where you headed?" Danita asked.

"To the liquor store, I might as well grab a buzz, and get dizzy since I'm dealing with this kindergarten game of merry go round. I'm going to hopscotch my ass across the street for some Sutter Home. You want to ride?"

I used those few minutes to let Danita know I was up on the game and that I wanted to give Darryl enough time to call Ricky to let him know he succeeded at keeping me away.

"His punk ass wasn't lost, and whatever is up in Orlando, I plan to find out when I get up in the morning."

# Chapter 18

"Ugh, who is that with Eric?" Danita asked.

"I don't know," I said. As we drove up closer to Eric's black Maxima, we recognized the other man as Ricky.

"Damn, that's Ricky," we both said.

Neither of us had ever seen Ricky unshaven. He looked like a different man. I looked at Danita slyly and rolled the window down.

"Let his nightmare begin," I whispered. "What's up fellas?"

"Hey what's up?" Ricky asked.

"Ricky I think you have a matter to settle with me," I said.

"Park and come on in," Ricky said. "When did you get here?"

I parked the car and walked up to him.

"What the hell happened to you?" I asked. "You look like shit."

"I told you I got injured. I had to have surgery," he said. "This is only my second time out of the house."

"Well, we can make this quick. I'm not here to get into how you are, and what you've been up to," I said. "Where is my money?"

"Come on in and let's talk in private," Ricky said.

When we walked inside, the apartment was a mess. A throw was on the sofa from where Ricky had been lying around. Fast food containers and beer bottles covered the dining room table. It was hard to believe this was the same clean apartment I was used to walking into. The place looked like a pig sty.

I followed Ricky to his bedroom where the bed was neatly made. Clothes from the dry cleaners were piled on the dresser. Big bath towels were lying on the bathroom floor.

"Where is my money Ricky?"

"Come here." Ricky tried to make a romantic moment and began to rub my thighs.

"Fool, this ain't no social call. It's fucked up that you're playin with my emotions over this Ricky," I said.

"I said I don't have it."

"When did I miss that?"

Ricky grabbed me and pushed me back on the bed and straddled on top of me.

"This will never be over," he said.

"You sound like a damn fool."

We wrestled, and I tried to get away. Ricky put a hold on me that I could not fight. He unbuttoned his blue jeans and lifted up my black mini skirt.

"You're crazy," I said. "Get the fuck off me!"

"This is my pussy, and I need to make love to you."

"This niggah, is my pussy and I should have been more like me and kept it to myself. I hate that I gave any to you," I said.

"Michelle you had that procedure done. Did you ask me? No, you told me. This was about more than just you."

"No shit Sherlock, it is about more than just me. I did what was right for me. I didn't have to ask you shit. You let me believe you were fixed. That lie canceled any fuckin right you had."

Ricky was holding my wrists tight. I couldn't even move my body for his weight. I knew I was fighting a losing battle. If I didn't give in he was clearly going to take the ass.

"Let me ride," I said. I knew I could turn him into a minute man if I rode him with the right rhythm. I straddled him like I was climbing on a horse and rode him to a quick climax.

When I came out of his bathroom I couldn't hide the hurt and disappointment that covered my face, and I couldn't fight the tears.

"If I had known what a stupid fuck you were, I would have ran the other way when I met your sorry ass. This is not the behavior of a man."

"I didn't tell you to get an abortion. You did that on your own."

"Yeah, I paid for a stupid ass lie you told." I headed for the bedroom door.

"Where are you going?"

"I'm going to the mall," I said

"Are you coming back?"

"I'll be back if I feel like it. A hotel would cost me a pretty penny, and I don't feel any change," I said. "You would want to listen very carefully Ricky. You have a debt that's about more than money, and you're right, it won't end. Just don't let the evil of the money trap your ass. When you see me niggah, you betta holla at me."

# Chapter 19

The mall was packed like sardines. Racks filled the walkway for the sidewalk sale. Danita was shopping seemingly until she was ready to drop. After walking through half the mall, we stopped at the pay phones. When Danita called Darryl he was acting flaky for some reason, and Ricky didn't answer his phone.

I was in a funk, but Danita continued to shop. Finally we headed for our last stop, Victoria Secret.

"Let's go see what they have," Danita said.

"The same secrets they always keep," I said. "Danita, I have to go back."

"Why? If Ricky sort-of raped you as you put it, cancel his ass."

Danita picked through the rack of g-strings. I had never stepped foot in Victoria's and not picked up a little secret. I was just not myself. Me, Miss Bargain Hunter USA, never even explored a sale rack.

"Danita, you have to trust me. I don't know what it is, but I have to go back."

"It's your call. I just think that Ricky is a sorry fuck. Darryl is acting flaky all of a sudden, practically hanging up on me, then you call Ricky and there's no answer. I know Ricky's punk ass called him right after we left. Darryl was cool when we left this morning, and now he's trippin. The punk probably told him I was in Eric's room, but I'm sure he never mentioned the door being open."

"You know I'm not trying to make Ricky my man. I am working on a feeling that is consuming my soul. I have to roll with it."

"Let's go."

The night skies in Orlando were beautiful. The soft air blew a light breeze on our skin. After filling the gas tank we picked up a twelve pack of Michelob, stopped at Popeye's chicken, and headed back to Ricky's.

My timing always seemed to be right on the money. Eric was pulling into a parking space just as we pulled in the apartments. A woman and two kids were getting out of the passenger side of his car. I parked right next to Ricky's truck behind Eric.

"What's up yall?" Eric called out.

"Nothing," Danita said.

"This is Rhonda," Eric said. "This is Michelle and Danita."

"Hey," I said.

"Are yall going out tonight?" Eric asked.

"Yep," Danita said. "Do you mind if we get dressed here?"

"No, never that," Eric said.

Rhonda was petite and cute. Her hair was jet black and she wore it in a short tapered cut like she was going for a replica of Halle Berry's look. She wore blue jeans and a pink sweater. Her little girls wore large jackets that hung off their shoulders. They took off running up the stairs to the apartment.

Eric reached around the little girls to unlock the door. The apartment was dim and quiet. Ricky walked out of his bedroom fully dressed wearing his gym shoes.

Eric broke the silence and turned on the TV. Danita and I sat down at the dining room table and started to eat our chicken, I opened a beer.

"Have a beer," I said.

Eric walked over to the table and picked a beer out of the box. Ricky got a beer, sat on the sofa, picked up the remote control, lifted his leg with his hand and planted it on the table.

"Hey man, the Magic are playing," Eric said.

Ricky turned to the Magic and the Bulls. I changed seats so I could see the television.

"What are yall doing, going out?" Ricky asked.

"Yep," I said. "We're taking off from there. Danita left some things at Darryl's and our flight leaves early in the morning. I think it's at 6:15 or 6:45, isn't it D?

"I think it's 6:45," Danita said.

"Anyway, by the time we get to Palm Bay and back after the club, we plan to stop for breakfast before we go to the airport," I said.

Ricky had a slight attitude, but I ignored it and him. He kept asking us when we were leaving. Danita kicked me under the table to get my attention and nodded toward Ricky.

"Ricky, did you want to settle with me?" I asked. I got up and threw away my chicken box and cleaned off the table. I turned up my Michelob, threw the bottle in the trash and opened another one.

"Do I want to what?"

"Settle with me," I said.

"Can I talk to you for a minute?" Ricky asked. He got up

from the sofa and headed to his bedroom.

"What's up?" I asked.

"You are so consistent," Ricky said.

"What? You should try not to be so persistent about not giving me the money you owe me. If you are ready to settle this, just pay me and I'll be on my way. Otherwise, I guess you will have to put me out forcefully."

"Michelle, I'm going to stop fucking with you. How do you know I didn't have plans?"

"Handle your business. I told you I want to get paid. If you want me to leave then take a quick trip to the ATM. If you don't have anything else to talk about I guess this conversation is over. Excuse me I have to kick it now."

I pushed him aside and walked out the bedroom door. Rhonda was on Eric's lap talking to Danita. I walked over to the sofa, and one of the little girls stood to her feet, stepping on one of mine on accident.

"Mommy can we see Eric's room now?" she asked.

I sat next to Danita on the sofa. "Recap real quick Eric," I said. "And please keep it consistent."

Eric gave me a recap of the game. Ricky came out of his bedroom and sat down.

Danita needed curling irons and Rhonda offered the use of hers. She and Danita took the rental car and left to go to her apartment to get them.

Eric jumped to his feet, seemingly relieved Rhonda was off his lap. He walked into his bedroom and called out for me.

"Come here Michelle I have a song I want you to hear," Eric said.

Eric and I had the same taste in music, so I knew he had something that I would be feeling. I stood in his doorway while he got the song set up on his stereo. Ricky rolled his eyes at me. I rolled my eyes back at him. "You know Ricky the money would walk me right out that door," I said.

"Whatever," he said.

Eric handed me the earphones to his stereo and I put them on. The song was not quite my taste at all. It was a song about a woman who is asking herself why she wants a certain type of man.

"Can you get with that?" Eric asked.

"It's Okay," I said. I waved my hand in the so-so motion while I read the CD case. "I don't like beggin music and I hate pity parties."

I noticed Ricky walking to the kitchen from the corner of my eye and felt him looking in the room at us. Eric must have felt like he was invading, so he turned off the stereo. We went back into the living room to watch the rest of the game.

Danita came back in the apartment alone with a pair of curling irons in her hand. "Your Mom said to come on. She drove her own car back," she said to the little girls. They grabbed their coats and headed out the door.

"Is your girl leaving you without saying good-bye?" I asked.

"She'll call when she gets home," Eric said. "I'm sure she wants to get the girls in bed."

Thirty minutes later the phone rang, I was sitting closest to it so I answered it.

"May I speak to Ricky?" the female voice asked.

I handed the cordless phone to Ricky. His end of the conversation made it obvious it was a female who was calling him out. He fussed for a minute before finally hanging up the phone without saying good-bye.

"That's over," he said.

"Ricky, you are going to end up a very lonely man if you don't let someone inside," I said.

"I can't have you the way I want you, so what does it matter?"

"You're right about that. I am not to be had by the likes of your sorry ass," I snapped. "Go out. I'm sure a big menu of pussy is waiting to be found at the club."

"I might just go out and get me some pussy," Ricky said.

"Go for it," I said. "Just stop telling that damn lie about being fixed, would you?"

The hostility between me and Ricky took center stage. I guess our performance wasn't winning any reviews. Eric walked over and turned on the stereo. Danita covered her mouth like she was in a state of shock, and that gesture only gassed me up.

"Until you know who you are you'll keep a taste in your mouth for something and you'll never figure out what it takes to satisfy your craving," I said.

"Whatever," Ricky said.

I knew the floor was mine by the look on Ricky's face. "You want a hot, small, square, go see Krystal. Maybe Wendy, she might be a little old fashioned, but you can have her your way," I suggested. "Heck, take a trip to a Dairy Queen, at least you can get a good lick. When you get home and lay in bed with a hunger that just won't quit, you'll think, I Hopped my ass from here to there, I'm broke, busted and disgusted, and he's still Hard--EES up on a brotha! What do you want, niggah what?"

"Fuck you Michelle."

"No, fuck you. You don't behave like a man, your bad. While you're doing all this indulging without using your thinking cap, one might blow up literally. You better be careful about sticking your Ding Dong in all kind of Ho-Hos. You might find out your Suzy-Q or your little Debbie got some stale stuff," I said. I pointed to his crotch. "That poor thing don't know shit about decision, but I'm sure he'll rise for any occasion."

Ricky stormed out of the room and went to shower. He came out of his bedroom dressed to go out, shaved and smelling good.

"Ooh baby you look tasty. Go rock that world around you, since that's what you're connected to," I said. "Be careful it can be dangerous putting raw meat on your grill, so wrap it up. Oh and Ricky, keep them molded buns off your polish sausage, it's unhealthy."

Ricky slammed the door and left.

"Damn that was backwards," I said. "Wasn't I supposed to get put out? Eric, wouldn't you just give me the money and rid yourself of the torture?" I asked.

"Michelle you are a trip," Eric said.

"Damn skippy," I said. " This is a trip his ass would want to take. Who else is going help him grow some balls and deal with his situations like a man? When you act like a child you get treated like one. He is at a kindergarten level when it comes to connecting with me. Damn, I must've been on some strong dope."

"Girl, just think that would have been your baby daddy," Danita said.

"I think he really wants you in his life Michelle, but you are very different," Eric said.

"I like the word misunderstood," I said.

"I think he is willing to do anything to keep you in his life," Danita said.

"Girl just think of how much more fun we have when Ricky's not here," I said. "How come I couldn't meet somebody like you Eric, who has connect ability?"

"Just don't let Ricky stop yall from keeping in touch with me," Eric said.

While Eric and Danita got dressed to go out, I left to go see Scott.

When I returned a little after three in the morning, Eric answered the door. Danita was nearly asleep on the couch. Ricky's truck was outside, so I assumed he was in bed. I waited for Danita to gather her stuff and we dashed out the door.

We were almost to the last step when I heard a door close.

"Michelle," Ricky said.

"Yes Ricky?"

"Come here for a minute," he said.

Danita turned around and headed back up the steps. "Come on Michelle," she said. "I'd rather lay on the couch than sit in the car."

We walked back upstairs and Ricky was standing right outside the balcony. I followed him to his bedroom.

"Michelle what are you doing?"

"What do you mean what am I doing?"

"You leave here and come back at three in the morning?"

I looked at my watch. "Actually, it's three fifteen."

"It's that niggah Scott isn't it?" Ricky pulled his jeans off and I stood with my back leaned on the door.

"I told you who Scott was to me. I have no reason to be dishonest with you. What would I gain from telling you a lie?"

"Okay, so I made a mistake. Ever since you had that abortion, all I hear you say is pay me, pay me. Look at me. When is the last time you talked to me?"

"All I see past what the naked eye revealed, is a naked ass."

"I don't just want to see you for sex."

"Ditto. We don't vibe. I am very mental Ricky, and I want a spiritual connection."

"You don't realize how many women would love to be with me."

"Good, then why are we having this conversation?" I asked. "Ricky, we are obviously not compatible, so why are we spinning the wheels?"

I reached for the door knob. Ricky rushed over and leaned over me.

"Let Danita drive to Palm Bay. Stay here, and let's just lay here and talk."

"Ricky can you please move?"

"Michelle, I want to get to know you, but I need for you to stop being so dominating and smart assy. I don't ever know what to say to you anymore. All you do is talk about money."

"You make my mouth smart. There is not another person I'm around who I talk sarcastic shit too. I might talk about money, but I'm not digging for gold. That abortion was a traumatic experience for me," I said. "Ricky if you want a trophy, I'm not the one. When I look at you, I don't see the glow that could turn me out. You should have looked beyond this cover, because there is a lot more to this book."

"Michelle, if that's the case, why did you get involved with me to begin with?"

"Ricky, I don't know right now, but I guarantee the reason will reveal itself to me in due time."

"I knew I should have walked away a long time ago."

"You walked after you got the ass."

"You're always saying shit in riddles to me. Talk straight."

"It's not my style. I can't teach you the things I've learned, but I can hint the things you need to pay attention to," I said. "Love can be a beautiful thing, but it takes time to develop. Real love can't begin until the infatuation stage has ended, and it does end. Relationships are created with strategy. If you want to reach the heights with it, you need to play the hands you are dealt, one at a time. Most of them are stepping stones, learning tools. The goal is to come to a draw when you find your treasure. You have to know when to hold them, and know when to fold them. We don't make a good pair. My hold card is wild, but I'm no joker."

Ricky lifted his hand from the door, closed his eyes, and shook his head. He dropped his heavy body across the bed.

# Chapter 20

I walked in my office Monday morning and was greeted by a tall stack of work in my basket that I had conveniently forgotten about. I sipped my steaming coffee and turned on my computer. My E-Mail was flooded. I started opening and answering it to get the day under way. When the phone rang, I noticed I had voice mail messages.

I took the business call, and then checked my messages. All business, and one lonely personal message was among them. It was Scott, he sounded excited about the material I had left for him to review over the weekend, and he wanted me to call him as soon as possible. I opened my desk drawer and pulled out my letter opener when something came over me.

A thought about the weekend was on my mind. Danita had mentioned Rhonda smoking when they were outside and Eric hates cigarettes. Miss Curious was very inquisitive about me, and shared with Danita that Ricky had a different girl over every time she visited. I stood up and made my way to the bathroom. I walked in the stall and sat down on the seat.

Ricky probably didn't know I was on my way to Orlando, if he did he would have been gone. I realized that Ricky wasn't out of town every time I had come, and Eric had a reason for wanting me to listen to that song. Rhonda was not Eric's friend, she was Ricky's. That had to be her who called when Ricky announced that was over. She was mad because he couldn't get rid of me!

I made my way back to my office and called Danita.

"Girl, why did I just realize that Rhonda was Ricky's company."

"What?" Danita asked. "You know what, Eric was rolling his eyes when she was sitting on his lap."

"Eric hates cigarettes, and she smokes. Her little girls knew exactly where they were going when they got out of the car, but one of them asked if they could see Eric's room now. That was because their mom was sitting on Eric's lap. Why would she ask to see Eric's room if they had obviously been there before? Eric played a song for me that was about a woman questioning herself about wanting a no good man. He meant Ricky, and was trying to tell me without saying it. Rhonda called after she got home to end it with Ricky because of me, and Eric never got a call."

"How did you figure that out?"

"It just makes sense. Have you ever seen Eric sweat a female? Why would Ricky have a sudden change of heart? Darryl didn't get in touch with him until we went to the mall."

"You might be right. Why don't you call Eric and ask him?"

"There's no need," I said. "I will be letting Ricky know that I'm not stupid."

"This drama is like a soap opera. I guess that would explain why Darryl wanted to keep you out of Orlando."

"Precisely," I said. "I was never out to salt Ricky's game, I use a little accent, because it wakes up my flavor. If he was open and honest liked he vowed to be, there would have been no need to worry. I never would have blown his cover, I know how to be on the DL better than R Kelly."

"What about the green light he gave you?" Danita asked.

"You know D, I expected a flow of traffic but he put me in the rush hour. He could have given a warning instead of trying to throw up a stop sign. That behavior was a mind blowing decision that you see caused a head on collision. It was not up to me to decide which way to go, if he were someone else's, all you had to do was let me know."

"How could he mistake you for a fool?"

"You can't slick the slicker. I guess he was about to make a mad dash, and was home free until old Michelle was at the door when it opened," I said.

"No wonder Rhonda wanted to know more about you. But you know me, I defined your flavor to her just like you would have," Danita said. "And she claimed Eric was always blowing up her pager, begging her to see him."

"I've been around Eric more than I've been around Ricky and I've never seen him sweat a girl," I said. "Most niggahs don't know shit about that thing called timing, it's an incredible thing to try and understand, but this one holds the keys to a success story. There were kids in the background the night he played me off on the phone. Play me? No, he played himself, but I play it best. Two wrongs don't make it right but it damn sure makes it even."

"The saga continues," she said.

"Yep," I said. "It will do just that. I won't stop until I hear the fat lady sing. I gotta go, I'll talk to you later."

The unfolding drama was on my mind the entire day. On my way home I thought again about this feeling like an ongoing movie. There was never a doubt in my mind that there would be a dream that defined the weekend. As soon as I got home, I walked in and winked at Jesus. I went upstairs to review my journal. Sure enough there were two dreams that redefined the moment in question.

♠

*Who's Michelle*

*Danita and I are at Ricky's. We leave and get in his truck. Danita and I climb in the back seat. There is a girl in the passenger seat, who tries to place her hand on the back of Ricky's head. He tries to stop her. We get out of the truck and go back inside. The girl suddenly wants to know which one of us is Michelle. I tell her it's me and she asks me to step outside. Ricky asks me if I am going to screw around because he did.*

♣

*What's Up With That?*

*Me and Danita are pulling in Ricky's complex. Eric and a girl are walking up to the apartment. I walk behind Eric and ask him what's up with her. He calmly says, nothing. Ricky is inside. Him and the girl are both trying to swallow a ring, she is gagging. Ricky has trouble swallowing his, so the girl kisses him and blows it down his throat Everyone except me starts to do the electric slide. I awake.*

# Chapter 21

I arrived in Orlando on a Friday to a muggy day where the remnants of rainy weather were clinging to the air. I started to feel like I lived between two cities when the faces of travel attendants and rental car agents were becoming familiar. I never thought I would dread looking at a city I had once loved so much.

I-4 was busy with evening commuters when I merged into traffic in a rented SUV. I stopped at a liquor store to pick up a fifth of Remy before I checked into the Holiday Inn in Winter Park.

I dropped six ice cubes in a glass from the vanity, and poured myself better than a two shot drink of cognac. I turned on the TV, and switched to CNN. I turned up my glass, and swallowed the strong liquor that made my face frown. I piled more ice in my glass, and poured another strong drink to sip on.

I turned the air conditioner to a cooler setting to freshen the dry air and plopped down on my stomach on the cozy double bed.

I thought about Scott, and reached over to the small night stand and picked up the telephone receiver. He had no idea I was coming in town, so when I got his voice mail, I left a message with the hotel and room number for him to call me back.

When hunger struck, along with a serious buzz, I left the room to go to Popeye's, my favorite food stop in Orlando. As soon as the door closed behind me, I realized I left my key card on the dresser.

I took a long walk to the lobby since all entrances except the front door were kept locked at night. I stood near the sofa situated between two tall tropical plants and gazed out the window while I waited for an elderly couple to check in. The front desk clerk didn't wait for me to finish my request before she started to code me another key.

Night had almost completely fallen when I exited in Altamonte Springs. The heat had dried up most of what was left of the rain. When I pulled into the lot of the restaurant, a car pulled up behind me flashing their brights. I turned to see who was trying so hard to get my attention, but couldn't see for the light shining in my face. My heart thumped so hard I felt the beat in my ears.

I opened the door, jumped out of the cab, and shielded my eyes from the headlights with my hand. A tall man walked through the beaming light, and approached me.

"Hey Michelle," he said.

"Eric?" I said "You scared the shit out of me. I thought you were a cop."

"I saw you back there at the light. You pulled up right next to me. I tried to get your attention, but you were too into your music," he said. "I just left the mall."

"You recognized me in the dark?" I asked.

"I only noticed you because I saw you fluffing your hair in the rearview mirror. I thought you might be some sister I would want to meet. I knew for sure it was you when you pulled in Popeye's. What are you doing here?"

"Our place got broken into Monday. I flew in to get some stuff to replace what we lost," I said.

"Damn, that's messed up."

"Tell me about it. Danita may've walked in on them. She came in and found the back door standing wide open. My computer was on the floor in front of the stove, and you know how important my writing is to me. It's hard to swallow. They were seconds away from taking my whole life. I am so thankful they didn't get my computer," I said. "It was awful. They even rummaged through our dresser drawers. The thought that someone's hands were on my panties makes me sick."

"Let me park and come in."

I turned off the ignition and got my purse. I thought about how preposterous it was that I would run into Eric. If I didn't know any better, I would have thought I was being followed.

"Are you going out tonight?" Eric asked.

"No," I said. "I want to be rested enough to leave tomorrow."

"Does Rick know you're here?"

"After our last encounter, I haven't thought much about being with a man like that," I said. "Wasn't that what you tried to tell me the last time I was here?"

Eric shook his head. "You can say that."

We both ordered spicy chicken, and Eric ordered some red beans and rice. We went to a table in the back of the restaurant near the window.

"So I guess that means you're not staying at our place."

"Hell no," I said. "I checked into a hotel."

"Do you need some help loading the truck?"

"Yes, that would be nice Eric. I want to go work out after I check out of my room," I said. "I'll be ready after that."

"Go to the gym with me," Eric offered. "I work out every Saturday morning. You can pick me up and we can leave from there to load the truck."

When I woke up the next morning, I called Eric from the hotel to let him know I was on my way so he would be ready.

After a hard workout, we loaded my TVs, VCRs, family photos and some wall art into the truck. I tried to fit everything that meant something to me, so that I wouldn't have to come back to Florida for a while. After all these months in the cramped, dry space, my furniture was practically ruined.

By the time I drove Eric home, I felt so hot and sticky that I decided to come up and take a shower before I hit the road.

It was obvious by the startled look on Ricky's face that Eric didn't mention my being in town. Ricky was sitting on the sofa with a man dressed in a gray suit.

Papers were spread out over the coffee table. Ricky stood up, walked over, and gave me a kiss on the cheek.

"Hey Michelle," he said. "Why didn't you tell me you were coming? This is Randall Smith." The nerdy man stood and offered his hand to me.

"It's nice to meet you," I said.

I followed Eric to his bedroom. He stepped in his walk-in closet and came out holding some fresh towels.

I was standing at the fogged mirror brushing my hair when I heard Randall giving Ricky some specs on a condo. I walked over to the closed door and held my ear open to hear the conversation. Randall quoted Ricky's salary from the Predators, and asked him how much he made driving the school bus. I turned and wiped the mirror with the towel and finished my hair. I cracked the door to let in some cool air and put on my black sweat suit.

When I walked out, Eric was making his bed. His bedroom door was wide open, which I'm sure was out of respect for Ricky. The white muscle shirt he wore clutched the fierce six pack on his glowing bronze skin. His black gym shorts gripped his thick thighs. His cut calves, barely hairy, were well defined by lines of toned muscle. Eric was one fine hunk of a man.

"Thanks Eric," I said. "I feel so much better now. I don't know what I would have done without you."

"It was my pleasure Michelle," he said. He walked over and gave me a hug and an innocent kiss on the cheek. I inhaled some of his cologne, and resisted hugging him passionately. I grabbed my duffel bag and headed toward the door.

"Where are you going?" Ricky asked as he stood to his feet.

"I'm on my way home," I said. I looked at Randall. "It was nice meeting you."

"Michelle what are you.. when did you get here? I need to talk to you," Ricky said. "Hold on for a minute. This is only going to take another few minutes."

"No. I'm sorry Ricky," I said. "I want to get home before it gets too late. Why don't you call me?"

Eric walked in the living room, reached around me and opened the door to walk me outside. When we got downstairs I turned to him. "Surely he didn't think he was about to get another piece of ass," I said.

"I think he thinks he's in love with you Michelle," Eric said.

"I think that I could have more likely fallen in love with you," I said.

Eric opened the back door of the truck, moved some boxes around, and put one in the passenger seat. "Now maybe you can see out the rearview mirror."

"Thanks Eric," I said. I crossed my arms, leaned back on the driver's side door, and looked around at the beautiful scenery. I took in a deep breath and let out a long sigh. "For some reason, I get the feeling this may be the finale to the saga."

"You have to be the most incredible woman I've ever met Michelle," Eric said. "If there is any person I can say who has everything it takes, it's you."

"If I hadn't needed that final key," I said shaking my head.

"What?" Eric asked.

"Nothing. I just thought that I wouldn't have seen you if I hadn't needed to get another key last night. Everything truly does happen for a reason," I said. "It was really nice knowing you Eric. It's not everyday that you meet a person who can connect. I just hope that one day you understand all of this drama."

"I can't put words to what it is about you," he said.

"I'm sure it's no secret to you, and I know I can safely say, I am very attracted to you."

"We do have a lot in common."

"A lot more than words can describe," I said. I climbed in the cab, turned the ignition on and rolled the window down. "There's just no right way to do something wrong."

“Between me and you, Ricky has said sleeping with you is like dope. I guess it gets him high,” Eric said with a chuckle.

“That is funny. Leave it to him to use an anatomy like that,” I said. “I know I can lead, but I wouldn’t call it a drug. The treatment I push is from within. If he spoon fed instead of injecting himself, he could’ve capitalized.”

We both laughed.

“I’ve read some of your stuff, and it would be intimidating to most men. It’s some deep ass game girl,” Eric said.

I put on my sunglasses, and adjusted the rearview mirror. “That’s just it Eric, life is a game, and the only way to get ahead is to strive to become a carbon copy of the soul.”

“You do plant a lot of seeds,” he said.

“I do it only when growth is required in order for me to gain from the experience. You know you’ve got a long way to go if I start a garden.”

"As much as I want to kiss you," he said. "I can't do it to Rick."

"I know," I said. "I feel the same way. “I wish you the very best Eric.”

# Chapter 22

Life was flowing in robotic routine like a marching band. I found a new gym that was open twenty four hours where I worked out on a regular basis. I was continuing to love the life I was making for myself in Nashville. I was writing and dreaming constantly.

When the Friday after Valentine's day rolled around, I wasn't in the mood for any liquor or company. I wanted to seclude myself from everything. I left work early enough to have the place to myself for some time to devote to my inner spirit.

After a couple of hours of prayer and meditation I made my way to the kitchen for some water to quench my thirst. Once I finished my bottled water, I retreated back to my bedroom for more meditating before the phone broke my moment.

I was in one of my infamous moods of just not wanting to be bothered by anyone. I was in bed and refused to get up when Danita came home. I was determined to make some time for myself. I felt like I needed more than just quiet, I needed some inner peace. I went deep in serene and fell asleep and was finally taken in deeper than I had ever been before in a dream that rates as one of my most intense ever.

When I awoke Saturday morning I made my way downstairs and started a pot of strong coffee. I filled my favorite coffee mug and put it on the coffee table while I went upstairs to get my journal and tape recorder.

I opened the blinds and let the window up just enough for

some cool air to seep through to freshen the air. I sat on the couch in my terry night pants and matching sleeveless shirt, and curled my legs under me. I rewinded the tape I recorded after my dream and listened to my groggy voice telling of the experience I had the night before while I recorded the experience in my journal.

"It felt like I was pulled into a very deep sleep. It sounds like an older car pulls up in the driveway. It sounds like a real old car. I hear the gears shift, attached to the steering panel, move from drive and clicking its way into park. The motor turns off. I feel someone grab my hand and lead me into a dream where I am an onlooker standing in the distance. My mother is outside a mansion sweeping the sidewalk that is adjacent to a park. I wonder why she is sweeping because I don't see any dirt or dust. She looks like she did in her younger years. A man walks down the steps from the mansion taking long strides toward her in a tan, seventies style suit with a piece of paper in his hand. When he gets closer to her, I notice that the paper in his hand has my signature on it seven times. My mother and the man are communicating but their mouths aren't moving. I feel like he is telling her that I was easy to work with and that the job was a success. I feel like my signature is an acknowledgment of work being done, like an assignment. I awake."

I sat in the silent room and finished recording the dream that I titled, Mission Accomplished. I prayed a prayer of thanks for the dream, which was the first dream I had of my mother since she passed away where I got a good look at her.

I laid on the couch and closed my eyes. Before I knew it I had dozed off and was in another dream, the most remarkable of my life.

♦

*This Is Your Life*

*I am at the house where my mother last lived. I am picking up the pieces to a puzzle. I hear some excitement going on outside and walk over to the door. People are gathered in the large field across the street. I open the door and notice that they are all amazed because it is thundering and snowing at the same time. I walk down to the corner. The lights from the college that are shining bright like there might be a game going on at the ball field. I see a brighter light in the sky that twinkled with gold. The light is slowly coming closer and it begins to take form in an oval shape, with the gold light shining around its edges. Jesus is standing in the light. I admire Him while I wave hello, He waves back at me. His hair is brown and wavy, and He has a beard and mustache. He is wearing a pearl white robe and has gold glowing sandals on His feet. He looks slightly different from the famous pictures. Suddenly I am distracted by a movie screen that appears on the side of the post office building, where a movie with three black women is playing. I think of Waiting to Exhale. I turn and walk back toward the house, I no longer see anyone in the field. I awake.*

Was I losing my mind? I had to register the dream again. Why did I turn around? Why didn't I stay there to admire Him? Why was everyone suddenly gone? I closed my journal and looked up in the direction of the TV where I noticed a note from Danita. She had gone out to breakfast with Justin.

On my way back to the sofa, the portrait of black Jesus above the mantel caught my eye. I looked at the other walls in the living room and thought about where I could move it so that it would be in better view.

I took a generic home interior print off the wall next to where the entertainment center was standing. I reached for the portrait and looked into the eyes of black Jesus that I had admired since the first day I came to Nashville.

The minute I touched it, I experienced an extraordinary sensation. It felt like a rush that was flowing like an electricity through my veins. I stood there in a state of complete shock. All of a sudden I could see events run rapidly through my mind that had taken place in my life over the last several months, like an electric slide show. My eyes were open. In between the flashes of the different scenes, I could see the portrait. The flashes of the movie in my head were unveiling a story before my eyes.

I held the portrait out with my arms, while my eyes lay glued to those of Jesus. Never once did my eyes move. My trance finally broke after several minutes. My body tingled with the same feeling you get when your arm or leg falls asleep. My mouth hung open, and my hands felt sweaty.

At last, after several seconds I moved my body from the spot where it froze and hung the portrait. I stood with my arms held out while the tingling sensation I was feeling continued for more than another minute before it faded away. I felt like I was about to pass out on the floor. I picked up the cordless phone and dialed Danita's cell phone number.

"Danita, whatever you are doing can you please come home as soon as you can?" I asked.

"Is something wrong?"

"No, I can't even get into it over the phone, but I have to tell you about it."

I hung up the phone without realizing I hadn't said good-bye. I had never felt a rush like I just did. I grabbed a pen and notepad out of the kitchen junk drawer and started to write my feelings down as quickly as my hand would go. I threw the pen down and turned my computer on. My fingers pecked at the keyboard seemingly on their own.

When Danita walked in the door I was still typing at full speed looking at the monitor as the words spilled across the screen.

"Danita, you are not going to believe what just happened to me," I said. I raised up from my desk chair in the dining room and walked with her into the living room. I slowly sat on the couch still feeling an after shock from the episode.

"It all started last night when I had an incredible dream about my mother. I came down here this morning, and had an even more incredible dream where I saw Jesus. After I woke up, I oddly decided I wanted to move that portrait from the wall above the fireplace over here. When I touched it, I experienced a rush like sensation. After that, these flashes of things that have happened in my life recently kept flashing before my eyes," I said.

While I told her about This Is Your Life, she sat across from me with her mouth wide open. I knew she didn't know what to say.

"If I were anyone else, you would think I was crazy wouldn't you?" I asked.

"No, there are more things that can't be explained than can when it comes to the Lord Michelle."

"I want you to listen to this dream I had last night."

I rewinded the tape and played it back for Danita. She sat back on the love seat in slow motion while she listened to my dream.

"Oh my God Michelle. You're not going to believe this, but you know my dad died in the seventies and my last memory of him, well, he is wearing a tan suit."

I instantly felt chills run down my spine and if I had hairs on the back of my neck they were at full attention.

"Hold on a minute," Danita said. She ran up the stairs and came back down a few minutes later with a photo of two men and handed it to me. When I looked at it and I know my heart skipped a beat.

"This one is the man I saw talking to my mother," I said.

"That is my dad."

"But we didn't even know each other until just eight years ago."

"I know, but you dreamed about my dad," she said. "I wonder what this means."

I handed the photo back to Danita and walked in a daze to the kitchen. I didn't know what to make of the whole ordeal. Danita was just as dumbfounded as I was.

"Danita, please don't take offense, I know I asked you to come home," I said. "But I need to be left alone."

Danita hugged me. Tears were forming in the wells of her

eyes.

I sat in front of my computer writing non stop until it was time to go to work on Monday morning.

# Chapter 23

9 Months Earlier In Heaven

Bertha Cooper looked wide eyed as she and Kirk Neilson approached the big glass building buried in the snow white clouds. Bright gold glittery letters boldly stated its name, Heavenly Solutions. Bertha gazed at the beautiful building held up by the bright beautiful sky, her eyes filled with bliss.

The high tech office smelled like the clean sunshine. Inside, the office was filled with smiling angels diligently at work. Kirk and Bertha walked up to the welcome area in the middle of the large room. The beautiful receptionist, dressed in a snow white skirt, and matching blouse that was tailored perfectly, greeted the two of them with a huge grin.

"Hi Kirk," she said. "You must be Bertha, my name is Janice, right this way." It was apparent she was familiar with Kirk from the past, and was pleased to meet Bertha.

"It is a beautiful day filled with many blessings," Kirk said. He buttoned his suit coat as they proceeded to an open waiting area filled with gold thrown chairs. Janice's marble desk was centered in front of the waiting area, and shined like a brand new gold coin.

"Feel free to be seated. Make yourself at home," Janice said.

Kirk looked at his reflection as he stopped to admire the

wall of success. He motioned for Bertha, and showed her the great wall that validated the mastery of divine intervention. The theme was crafted with the images of successful seekers of a heavenly solution and their stories.

The etching of the bright gold sculpture continued to mold with great intensity by an invisible source. The constant changing work of art formed like hot wax being poured on a mountain of rocks.

The carved stone stretched down the hallway more than twenty feet. At the end of the ever growing wall, Kirk pointed out the two of them, their images as they appeared at that very moment. Like a piece of detailed pottery, the image of the two of them shaped into a mold like a mirrored image. The stone wall continued to grow with images, changing with every moment.

"When this is over," Kirk said. "Our images will either grow with the wall, or simply disappear."

When another man's image appeared on the stone next to their own, Kirk turned to greet Dexter Howell. The well built older man, dressed in a pewter gray, double breasted suit, and black tie rounded the corner smiling, extending his hand to Kirk. His six foot frame was shielded by an open trench coat. His salt and pepper hair was cut close and was topped with a gray fedora.

"God has truly blessed in fine ways," the man said.

"Yes, as always. How are you Dexter?" Kirk and Dexter shook hands. Bertha turned and walked over to the two gentlemen.

"Dexter Howell," Kirk said. "This is Bertha Cooper."

"It's nice to meet you," Bertha said. "It is amazing to me the countless number of forms we come in."

"The amazement never ends," Dexter said. "It's like the air you breathe is an inhaler of true fascination. I've been around here for nine years and I still get the intoxicating rush."

Kirk gave Dexter two pats on the shoulder when they neared the lounge where Janice was standing in front of her desk holding a file in a bright gold jacket. Her tight wide French roll, was a perfect contrast to her very sophisticated style. Her lavender nail polish twinkled in the bright light. Her long fingers danced along the edge of the folder. "Now that you are all here, I'll show you to Hearing Room A, your appointment is with the Honorable Adam," she said.

Janice led the way down the long hallway. The cathedral high ceiling gave off a soft echo to the sound of Janice's black pumps as she proceeded to escort the party down the glossy marble floor. They walked through an automatic glass door and into a courtroom setting where a table framed the raised bench of the arbitrator. A stenographer suddenly appeared at a table near the bench with her fingers in position to work.

The Honorable Adam walked out of his chambers. His white robe flowed as he walked up the steps to his bench. His teal green tie peeked through the collar of his robe. His appearance was neat and distinguished. Janice handed the file to Honorable Adam and walked out the glass door. The faint echo faded at her every step down the long hallway. Honorable Adam took his seat and took off his wire rimmed reading glasses.

"Good morning to all of you," Honorable Adam said. "Please be seated."

As the stenographer's fingers began to dance at the

machine, Honorable Adam opened the file and rested his reading glasses on his thin nose. The waiting angels were seated at the long polished table in front of the bench.

"We are here on this earth date of August 9, 2000. Bertha Cooper and Dexter Howell, you are here on behalf of your human loved ones and have filed separate claims in their interest. I have read your claims and processed them as you well know."

He took off his glasses and poured water from a glass pitcher into a small crystal glass. He directed his attention to the eager faces of the three angels in front of him.

"Bertha, you have filed a claim on behalf of your daughter Michelle Cooper. I see here in your claim that she was successful at unlocking her magic and has accepted that gift as her seed of purpose. In your claim you state that she is, in your opinion, ready and able to perform her talents in the interest of God.

"Dexter, you have filed claim on behalf of your grandson Ricky Howell to grant him the opportunity to enhance his career where there is greater fortune potential to share with the remaining Howell's. Is that correct?"

Dexter stood to address the arbitrator.

"Yes sir," he said. "My family has struggled for generations and have paid due after due. My son will be taken away from them very soon and Ricky has the talent to bring some fortune to care for his mother and other family members."

Dexter caressed his tie as he made his way back to his original seated position.

Honorable Adam began using his hands to express himself as he spoke.

"And you Kirk are here representing Bertha as her guide,"

Honorable Adam said. "Is that correct?"

"Yes sir, that is correct," Kirk said.

Honorable Adam took a drink of his water and continued as the three waited anxiously to find out why they had been asked to come together.

"It is very important that you all understand that these human souls will be put to a test. Each test has been designed to meet individual requirements and is in no way a competition. The tests have been approved by the forces of the Almighty. You are free to continue your daily works and dream delivery if you so choose. Do you understand?"

The three waiting angels all shook their heads.

They each replied, "Yes sir."

"Now Bertha, Michelle has been assigned to deliver Ricky's test and will be entering his life on earth tonight. Michelle's dreams will come true for her if she can make them unfold. The time limit on each of these tests has been limited to a period of one year. If the tests are not met in a satisfactory manner, the result will end in a no blessing situation. Any subsequent claims you understand, cannot be made for the period of one earth year. My role here is to simply acknowledge your claims and to make you aware of the tests and to address any concerns. Are there any questions?"

"No," Kirk said. He looked at Dexter and Bertha to make sure he wasn't answering for them. Bertha shook her head and Dexter again came to his feet.

"How do we know that Michelle will deliver the test to Ricky successfully?" he asked.

"That encounter has been staged and will occur, there is

no doubt it has already been written. The only thing that can alter it is divine intervention, and I don't think either of you would want to interfere with this test. I cannot disclose the specifics of the tests but I can assure you they are accurate and authentic," Honorable Adam replied. "Is there anything else?"

"No sir," Dexter said.

"Well then the best of luck to all of you." He raised up out of his chair picking up the file as he stood. "Share the blessings of the day."

In the hallway, Kirk held out his hand and grabbed Bertha's arm to stop her.

"I have to get to work. I have to take a trip. I don't want you to worry about this. I have my experience behind me and I don't have the time right now to show you the trade in detail. Just trust me okay?"

Kirk's experience in this life was twenty years strong and he felt good about the outcome.

"I trust you," Bertha said. Her eyes were as sure as her reply.

# Chapter 23

Two months had passed since my extraordinary experience. I left work early on Friday and headed to the airport to pick up Scott. He had been very insistent on seeing me, and I looked forward to having him there. The past several weeks we had been on the phone like we were neighbors.

I parked short term and walked inside the busy airport to find his gate number. His flight was scheduled to arrive on time. He walked through the chute wearing black shades and a new short afro. A bold silver chain hung around his neck on the outside of his black turtleneck sweater and small silver hoop earrings hung in his ears. His black jeans were fitting just right. A black leather briefcase was hanging on his shoulder and as always he smelled wonderful, leaving some of his mesmerizing scent on me from our embrace.

"How are you doing Miss Mysterious?"

"I'm good Scott," I said. "How have you been?"

"I'm real good now, look at you. This has to be the first time I've seen you in a nine to five look."

"Okay Scott, save the drama," I said. "I just got off work. What are you going for the Lenny Kravitz look? What's next, are you going to grow dreads?"

"Funny Michelle."

"No, it's quite right," I said. I shook my head in approval.

"It's working."

"Well I want to go somewhere where we can talk." I drove away from downtown and headed to Chili's in The Hermitage. The last hours of daylight were slowly fading away when we parked and walked inside. We were seated in a cozy booth in a corner of the restaurant. Scott was his same, sexy self. He finally took off his shades to reveal his very serious eyes.

"Girl, you are one talented individual. There was never a time that I didn't believe that deep down you knew you had something to do."

The waitress placed napkins in front of us. I ordered a margarita and Scott had his usual gin and tonic. When she came back with our drinks, she brought some chips and salsa that Scott dug right into.

"I can't tell you how much I value having you there for me. You are my best critic. I love what you are made of," I said.

"I think you have a lot of wonderful things to offer to a lot of people and I think you have the ability to make a positive impact on lives. You even touched a part of me that has me measuring my girls up to a new standard."

"I'm sure you have never had a problem finding a suitable nine or even a dime."

"Well the way I look at everything around me is somewhat different now, since we met."

"I'm flattered," I said. "But you know I've been known to be the smartest of asses."

"It's all good though," he said. "You know how you think of yourself as isolated, so much so, that you are afraid of what people will think?"

"It isn't that I don't want to share my work," I said. "I just know how hard I can be to take."

Scott ordered a sampler platter as usual and I asked for a petite sirloin with french fries. The dinner was tasty and the company was even better.

"I have something for you," Scott said.

"What is it?" I asked. "Don't tell me you are about to propose, I don't think I can handle that, we've never even kissed," I said.

"Quit being silly," he said. "I would have to grow too fast if I thought I wanted to keep up with a diva like you."

"Since that's out of the question, what is it?"

We both laughed. He opened his briefcase and took out a gift wrapped in simple paisley print gift wrap with a matching ribbon. I began to unwrap my present. I unfolded the taped edges one side at a time. I felt like a little kid on Christmas morning.

"Is this why you wanted to come?"

"Yes," he said. "This is not something I could have mailed and who knows when you will make it back to Orlando."

I finally pulled the paper apart enough to see a beautiful work of art, a professional manuscript that beamed the title of my vision, Visual Eyes.

My face lit up like a Christmas tree, the same way a little kid feels on Christmas morning.

"You can't skip out on your calling," he said. "I'm proposing myself as your literary agent."

I reached over the table and offered my hand to my new agent. We shook hands to seal the deal.

"You still have some work to do. I think we can wrap it

up over the next couple of days, I hope you're game for that."

"Are you kidding? We can dedicate your trip to the finishing touches."

"I've compiled all your work with the exception of any changes you may have made from my recommendations," he said. "And I'm still not clear on exactly what it is with Kirk," he said. "And what about Ricky?"

"Scott, I think Danita could bear the soul of my twin, there has to be a connection of some kind for Kirk to come to me. And Ricky, well, I truly believe that ordeal was about the both of us, not competitively, but I think we were both tested," I said. "I know we weren't brought together to be a couple, and you know everything happens for a reason. I don't think my pregnancy was about a life as much as it was about a situation. I'm not trying to justify my choices, but if there is a price attached for what I did, I know I'll pay it."

"There you go, going deep again," he said. "Do I need a life jacket?"

"I think my test was a matter of making those seven tools that I talk about with intense conviction, work for me. That is what I want to share. Life is like a game of recollection. A journey is followed by chips that will fall. They are scattered and hidden, but when you uncover one, you have to make the connection. I picked up the pieces and my story was unveiled," I said. "Scott, the very thought that I was touched by an angel feels like magic. I could have grown comfortable with repetition, and let my purpose in life pass me by, but I am determined to find my legacy. This tribulation came together for me from six feet under, and I'm ready for what's next."

"You are truly amazing," he said.

"When Ricky and I dined out, Reggie picked up the tab and he never followed through with paying for the rental car. The only thing Ricky bought me was a candy bar, and he handed me my payday, literally."

"You ordered a payday?"

"Yep, and I know I have told you about my parents. If there is a place in Heaven to take a gamble, my mother is right there. Only now I think the stakes are the results of the mastery of divine intervention. It would take some skill to work with odds like I'm sure there were," I said. "Scott how often have you heard about someone who makes a break right after losing a significant loved one?"

"I guess I never thought about it," he said. "Michelle you go deeper than no other."

"I guess I do. I think the dreams I had were like a dress rehearsal for what was to come for me."

"Your next project probably should be that tool box," Scott said. "So why do you think you came into Ricky's life?"

"I think I was appointed to deliver his test. I mean, who better to make a delivery like that than someone who is connected? It had to be the money, and it had to be about more than owing me," I said. "The last time I saw Ricky was at his apartment a couple of months ago. There was a man there going over his financial information with him for a home loan. I was in the bathroom and overheard him when he verified his salary from the Predators, and he asked Ricky how much money he made driving the school bus."

"Ricky is not a school teacher?" Scott asked. "Damn."

"I know that his destiny is not for me to judge, and I'm not trying to, but I do know he had a dream just like me. I think I passed his golden opportunity straight to him and he didn't make the catch. I don't think we'll ever see a player in the NFL named Ricky Howell, and a salary in the AFL doesn't even match what I make now. He clearly had the chance to cross over to his next level of spiritual growth that certainly would have been topped with a blessing, possibly his dream. I believe it may be too late for him, because this test is over. That debt has to be in collections because he will never see me again. I just hope he finds a way to pull his credibility report and somehow make it good."

Suddenly the sound of clapping hands sounded. A group of employees from the restaurant gathered at a nearby table and started to sing Happy Birthday to a patron.

"I see a signature ending," I said.

"I don't think it can get any better than this," he said.

I pointed to the table where the celebration was going on. Among those singing was an overweight worker with a warm smile on her face. When her eyes met mine, I shook my head. "My power source has a great sense of humor," I said. "I didn't think I would literally hear the fat lady sing."

And the rest as they say, is history.

That chapter in my life closed with a bang and several anticipated book signings. Who knows what tomorrow may bring for me? After an experience like this, I can wait with patience for what will come about next in my life. It just goes to show that with a connection that is locked in, it is worth staying tuned for. Don't take my word for it, just read, Hebrews 11:1.

I hope not to leave any stone uncovered. I hope and pray that time will not run out for me before I uncover the final piece, and solve life's greatest mystery, my purpose. I want this gift to stay with me forever. This is my story, and I'm sticking to it.

**My Strength, My Man**

My Man Is the Best Man; Whatever I Need He does What He
Can

I Never Have To Worry, For He Is by My Side Constantly,
Because You Know, I've Got the Best Man There Could Ever Be

We've Been Together for Quite A Few Years, And At Times I
Would Leave Him Alone, But through It All, His Door Is Always
Open Inviting Me Home

The Reason I Would Leave Would Not Be Of His Concern, As
Long As the Time Spent Away, a Lesson I Would Learn

You See, I Cannot Make It Without Him, He's Not Only My
Confidant, And My Friend, He's My Lord, My Savior, My
Strength, My Man

Deatra Taylor

From the author:

The content of this memoir defies rational thinking, but I believe the substantiality with all my heart. I believed from the start that this story had all the qualifications for the making of a good novel, but the fortune to be made was never my motivation. The desire of my heart was to share my testimony that I know could not be possible without my having been tested. With the exception of the obvious, this look inside my journal is a true confession of a chapter in my life.

As I walk this battlefield on the wining team, I am armed with my belief system, so evil, beware. I look forward to working with my greatest allies, so that the rest of my days can be dedicated to my destiny, and keeping the battle for hope alive. As the way to my intended path continues to be laid out in front of me, I know I will meet a lot more people through those close encounters of a different kind, who will play a part in the making of my personal legacy.

I pray that my blueprint for this journey will continue to be as obvious and intense as the deep, beautiful sky. This story came to me from six feet under, and I'm sticking to it. There is real magic hidden in all of us. We were not built to see the wonders working around us.

All glory to God.